I0625155

Ponytail

The Love for Revenge

By Dr. Pradip Chauhan

Published by hrcpublisher.com

Contact: hrcpublisher@gmail.com

Ponytail

The love for Revenge

This edition is Published on: 1st May 2016
Hrcpublisher
Contact@hrcpublisher.com
Hrcpublisher.in
Hrcpublisher.org

Disclaimer
This book is purely a work of fiction and all characters in the book are fictional. Any resemblance to real life characters, living or dead is purely coincidental. This book is not intended to hurt any religion, caste, race, country or individual.
No part of this book may be reproduced or transmitted in any form by any means, electronic or mechanical, including photocopying and recording, or by any information storage and retrieval system, except as may be expressly permitted in writing by the author.

Typeset in Book Antiqua by hrcpublisher, Gujarat

Dedicated to my parents

About the book

Ponytail- story of a businessman, who has spent his life for making money and becoming powerful. But there was love to distract him from his goal of life...

Section 1

Ponytail: The Love for Revenge

Today a year has passed since I last saw Tapasya. I can still remember the night she left me and this house. She had found lipstick stains on my shirt. She was livid and wanted an explanation. Even I had not noticed the stains-they were not even real lip marks; just lipstick stains! I had no idea where the stains came from. My explanation apparently did not work.

Chapter 1

Three years ago....

I met her when I interviewed her for the position of Marketing Head in my small textile company. Her confident look with tight ponytail, corporate suit and knee-length skirt was not sufficient to impress me. What impressed me was her attitude towards work, her sincerity and her past job experience. I selected her for the job from a pool of seven candidates. My firm was growing and was among the best run companies in the city. I had started my own business after completing MBA from the Indian Institute of Management, Ahmedabad at the age of 26 years with an investment of few lakhs of rupees.

When I recruited the lady, I was 29 years old and owner of a company with fifty crore rupees turnover that offered industry's best salary to competent candidates. Her CV mentioned that she and I were of the same age. It seemed her work and personal experience had taught her to market herself well. I have a knack for spotting requisite qualities in people and I was confident that with her communication skills she could sell anything.

She had worked hard and done well in six months to prove herself. She enjoyed good professional relations with her colleagues. We had frequent and to the point conversations related only to work. I was really impressed by her work and dedication to my company. For the past week I had gone through her work profile and her family background after the management recommended her promotion. Her parents were divorced and her father Mr. Ramakrishna was a reputed businessman. I decided to promote her after discussion with my HR head. I called Tapasya into my office to congratulate and inform her of her promotion as Managing Director of our new branch in a neighbouring city with a good hike in her salary.

****

Chapter 2

She entered my room wearing the smile of a salesperson. I asked her to sit. She looked stunning attired tastefully in formal wear that accentuated her perfect figure.

"Tapasya, you will be glad to know that we are going to expand our business."

"Congratulations Sir!" She possessed polished corporate manners that I could never nurture myself.

"I have recommendation of your name as the MD of our new branch in Surat. I think this promotion is a reward for your dedicated work and is also a great opportunity for you." She smiled again, but this time her smile was dry and charmless.

"It is my pleasure, but..." I was expecting her to be happy but her reaction left me bewildered. My eyes were fixed on her face questioningly.

"But what Tapasya?" I asked after a little pause.

"I want to work under you and want to learn more from you." Now this was expected as most employees show the same gesture of respect to their boss.

"You will work under me even after your promotion and therefore I don't think you should have any objection to this promotion. Do you?"

"No Sir! Thanks for considering me for this opportunity. I accept the promotion!"

"Here are the papers that you need to sign. You can read them carefully before signing; it is just a formality but necessary."

I did not see any liveliness on her face while she read the papers before signing them; she might be good at hiding her feelings.

I was transferring three other well-performing employees from the Head Office to the new branch. I decided to host a small farewell party along with the announcement of the new branch opening. The responsibility for the arrangement of the party was given to Tapasya. I was aware of the fact that we were aggressively growing our business.

We had a small chat about the party. I talked about the budget and about the expected number of guests for the party. It would be a small party and only office members with their family members were invited. She asked me to give her some time to manage everything because she was tied up in urgent work.

"If you are busy with your work, I can ask someone else to arrange the party."

"No, sir, I would be delighted to perform the duty." I could see she wanted to do it.

For a fleeting moment she let her guard down. I saw an expression that I have never seen before. I noticed her face for the first time. Tapasya was indeed beautiful. I do not remember if I saw a more mesmerizing face in my life. I think I set my gaze on her face tad too long. She had sharp features exaggerated with light makeup. Mascara and eyeliner made her eyes look large and dark. The red lipstick made her lips pouty and luscious. Her ponytail slithered down her slender neck. I hoped she did not notice my gaze.

And then suddenly my thoughts turned to Myself–I was not bad looking either! I had grown my hair during college days that grew up to my shoulders even as I settled into running a company. A trimmed beard completed my dashing *Dhoni* look. My body had responded to the strict regimen I put it to everyday. Two-hour yoga followed by meditation and weight exercises turned me into a five feet eight inches' tall handsome guy with bulging muscles and washboard abdomen. Girls liked what they saw and loved to flirt with me. I was a babe magnet alright. But my only focus was on growing the business. Everything else was secondary. Dating and flirting with girls could wait. The only time I communicated with women was in the business context. That day, I could not shift my gaze from her troubled pretty face.

"Sir, may I leave?" Her eyes caught me staring into her face. I was mesmerised by those eyes and lips.

"Tapasya, take this responsibility only if you're comfortable." I tried to give her an escape route.

"No Sir, it's OK." She still sounded unconvincing to me.

****

Chapter 3

I was a demanding and strict boss but I certainly was not heartless. I could often sense my employee's frame of mind. I was a boss who not only believed in target based work, but quality based work too. Additionally, my overachiever persona and my assertiveness was enough to keep any employee in control and terror. Maybe that was the reason Tapasya reluctantly said yes to arranging the party.

I called Ahmad and asked him to make arrangements for the party instead. Ahmad was also a truthful and meticulous employee. He was to be the Marketing Head after Tapasya's transfer. I revealed the purpose of the party, the invitees list, and the other plans already discussed with Tapasya in her presence. Ahmad asked me to allow him to leave early for making the arrangements; the plan was to arrange dinner in a banquet hall of a four-star hotel owned by my acquaintance. I allowed him to leave early but only after the big announcement was made in the office.

I had about 25 employees working in my office, although my manufacturing unit had around 100-150 employees. The party was only for the 25 employees and their families.

I came out of my office with Ahmad and Tapasya to make the announcement. "My dear colleagues, I am here to announce with a heavy heart that our very efficient colleague, Miss Tapasya, will no longer work here with us. This is not all; even our Finance Manager, Mr. Mansukhbhai, who has been working with us since the establishment of this young company, Quality Assurance Manager Mr. Krunal, and Manufacturing Head Mrs. Vrunda will also be leaving us along with Miss Tapasya."

I paused to watch the reaction on the faces of the team. Everybody was surprised. They knew some large changes would be taking place, but the scale of my announcement was unexpected.

I continued to have some more fun. "Deserving juniors of all these four are going to replace them and will take their position and pay perks. I am officially announcing Miss Tapasya, Mr. Mansukhbhai, Mr. Krunal and Mrs. Vrunda, as directors of our new branch in Surat and as they have already accepted the proposition, they will move to the new manufacturing unit in Surat next week." Loud cheers rang around the room. The promoted team members were congratulated and wished well for the new assignment.

As the cheers quietened, there was more good news for the team. I continued, "In addition, each employee of Prajwalit Ltd will be offered one unit share of the company this year."

The performance of my company was superb and every single employee dreamt of owning the company and partnering with me. I was disbursing 500 shares of my company among the employees.

The market value of each share was around 25,000 rupees and those guys were fortunate to get them at 1000 rupees each. This was a huge bonus for everyone and the applause did not stop for a long time.

I was not finished. I had to shout to make myself heard. "Silence please! And to celebrate this double bonanza, everyone along with their family is invited to a dinner party tomorrow evening. To let you prepare for the party, tomorrow has been declared a half day. Ahmad will notify you of the venue and the time of the party by this evening before you leave." There was an electric buzz in the office and everyone seemed thrilled.

This was the first time I had given such a big surprise to my employees.

****

Chapter 4

I came back to my office, removed my rimless glasses, and stretched back on the chair. Playing with my hair, I allowed my mind to drift to college days.

Exactly eleven years ago, after passing junior college, I got admitted into the engineering college. My father was a brave and honest police officer, and my mother, the most beautiful woman in my life, was a housewife. I loved my mother the most and competed with Papa for her Love-I always won! Some bad people had issues with papa and had threatened him several times to stay away from their nefarious activities. But papa was a brave, strong and honest police officer. He was six feet long, healthy and muscular man.

The same year when I completed my junior college, mummy had an accident and suffered serious brain haemorrhage. The accident was the handiwork of the same nasty characters. The doctor had prescribed an emergency procedure which would cost one hundred thousand rupees. Papa did not have that amount of money and we eventually lost mummy. Papa could not bear the loss of his beloved wife. He died of a heart attack immediately.

I lost both my parents on the same day. As the barber shaved my head I promised myself that I will make as much money as possible. I will not go through the helpless despair when the life of a loved one is on the line just because of insufficient money. The thought will drive me for my remaining life.

I also took an oath not to marry until I became the richest and the most powerful person in the world. So that I don't ever forget my oath, as a reminder I kept my hair long and never cut them shorter than shoulder length.

Papa had left behind a small house and few thousand rupees from his gratuity fund. I continued my studies. To pay for my college fees, I gave tuitions to school children. Government scholarships continued to fund 50% of my Management studies. I was quite sharp and did well in studies. Nothing else interfered in my studies and I stayed focussed. At the end of studies, I was able to save two lacs of rupees. I had mortgaged my parental home to borrow another eight lacs from the bank and started a small manufacturing company called Prajwalit Ltd. Fortune followed my hard work and business acumen and soon I climbed the steps to success. In a very short time I was in the list of promising young businessmen. Although I was not a big name to start with but soon everybody took notice of my business.

My ambition was much bigger and I wanted to grow even more. I had established my business well in Ahmedabad and now I wanted to go national. Maharashtra would be my first stop on the journey. Surat was quite close to Maharashtra and the branch in Surat would help me expand to Maharashtra and other states. The strategy and the expansion roadmap were well planned by research and finance department taking into account all the risks involved. An Initial Public Offering of Rs 1000 crores would help me raise enough money to take the company national. The Surat branch will be the first step to execute my plan.

****

Chapter 5

A knock on the door interrupted my thoughts. I opened my eyes. "Come in."

Ahmad entered the room quietly. Ahmad was dressed in a striped blue shirt with dark blue pants. He was an intelligent guy with short hair, and a sweet smile. He had good office manners and was always polite with his colleagues. I always hired efficient employees and a common theme that ran through them was that they followed a universal rule of formal clothes and office manners. I swear I had never forced them to do so, but almost all of them seemed self-disciplined. On the other hand, I never put on a suit or formal shirts. I was usually dressed casually in jeans and T-shirt. But my dressing sense was always dynamic and energetic.

"Sir, everything has been planned. The party will be held tomorrow evening at 7:00 pm in Hotel Alphonso. I have arranged for 150 persons since 140 are expected to come."

"Just confirm if the dinner menu is suitable for everyone. Take care of the people who prefer Jain food. And yes, you can come with your girlfriend too; you will have a great day tomorrow."

He blushed, "I don't have a girlfriend, but I do have a fiancée."

"She is also allowed; but not with her parents!" Ahmad's face turned red.

"Thank you, sir. May I leave now?"

"Sure, you can leave now. Announce the venue and time to everyone in the office."

It was already seven o'clock. I again called all four lucky future directors in my office.

"You can all leave now and make arrangements for your relocation. You will each be provided with company accommodation and you will take charge no later than next Monday. So you have about a week to finish up your work here and give charge to your substitute and do the necessary handing over. I want some specific work to be completed before you all leave. I have mailed you the list. I know you have a lot on your mind but those files and work are critical, so get them completed before next Saturday. Do you have any questions?"

"No, Sir." Everyone chorused.

"You may leave now."

I was merged with my work after all had left.

****

I changed myself from a businessman to a young and dashing man when I left the office. But beyond office I did not have a life. I did not have any close relatives and there was never enough time to hang out with friends.

Locking the office behind me I was surprised to see Miss Tapasya still working. She was completely unaware of me walking to her. I was really impressed by her concentration and dedication. But I did not like that she had not followed my instruction.

"Miss Tapasya, this is not the best place for night stay. I think your home will be better." I tried to play with words in which I was not an expert.

"Sir, I am really sorry. But the work you wanted me to complete tomorrow is..." she trailed off. I have always seen her in control. Tonight she seemed a little bothered.

I was sure there must be a good reason for her to stay this late. Something must be wrong.

"But...?" I wanted to know what was going on.

"I have lost the file and my full seven-day's work. I could not find the file when I came in this morning. Something went wrong with the computer and the file disappeared. I was doing the whole work again and will submit it to you before tomorrow evening." I have never seen her disturbed. She sounded incoherent and was visibly upset.

That file was quite important and very

confidential for me. The file held future plans for my company, including plans for the IPO. I had given that file to Miss Tapasya to analyse, estimate, and prepare a marketing strategy for my new venture– launch of female garments brand. She knew the importance of the confidential file.

Hiding my disappointment, I asked Miss Tapasya not to worry.

"It's all right! Relax, and don't worry about the deadline. You can take a few days more to complete the work. As far as the file is concerned, we have fairly elaborate and secure computer network. The file should not go anywhere. We don't want our future plans to fall in hands of our competitors."

"I am grateful to you, Sir."

"Now shut down your work. We need to leave and my stomach is growling."

She gave me a smile, thanked me again, and shut down her system. We locked the office and walked to the elevator. My office was on the fifth floor in a commercial area of Ahmedabad. The elevator brought us down to the ground floor parking lot. I unlocked my brand new black Renault Duster with the remote key.

"See you tomorrow, Miss Tapasya. Good night."

"Good night, Sir."

****

Chapter 7

Rain was still coming down gently. I opened the door of my car, turned on the ignition and started to drive out of the parking lot.

To my surprise, Tapasya was still standing in the parking lot looking lost. I noticed that there was no other vehicle in the whole parking lot except for my car. On most days I was the last one to drive out. I was not sure if Tapasya owned a car but with her salary she should be able to afford one.

I drove back to her, "Tapasya, what happened? Where is your car?"

"Sir, I just realised that I had given my car for service. It will be returned tomorrow morning."

I was not sure what to do. If I offered her a lift she might misconstrue my intentions. I waited.

"I had planned to take public transport. I guess I am too late for that. Maybe I will take an auto rickshaw." She was still incoherent and dazed. It sure was not her day.

Whenever girls are in trouble, they want men to offer the help. I could never understand, why they don't ask for help?

"And where do you reside?" I asked her.

"Satadhar, near Ghatlodia." It was almost 45 minutes away.

"I don't think any auto rickshaw will take you there. I live in Satellite. If you are okay I can drop you off." Her face lit up with a brief smile. I swear, if she had shown more drama, I would not have given her the lift.

"Thank you again, Sir." She took her seat.

I threw the gear, released the clutch and we were on our way.

"I think the rain might slow us down a little. I don't have much to talk about. If you want you can listen to the radio."

I turned on the radio and selected my favourite station. Golden oldies hour was playing delightful melodies. The wet road was reflecting the street lights. The red stoplights created shimmering images. I drove carefully.

"Sir, if you don't mind, may I tell you something?" She could not bear the silence after ten minutes.

"Sure, go on. I never mind if someone tells me the truth honestly."

"You are totally different from what I had anticipated."

"You must have thought I was kind of peculiar."

"No Sir."

"So you found me strange. Why?"

"I always thought you were reserved and aloof, especially around girls. But today I feel you are very caring and have more respect for you."

"If I had not offered you the ride you might have thought that I am an uncaring man, right?"

"Perhaps, yes! I really wanted you to offer me the ride." I smiled lightly. I was surprised how innocent and honest she was. In the office she looked totally professional and in command. She did have a vulnerable side and now she was opening up.

"Anyway, thanks for the appreciation!" I was saying things that I never used to.

She relaxed her body in the seat and removed the ponytail rubber band. Her hair cascaded down to her shoulders. She took a sip from her water bottle.

"Do you want a sip?"

My throat was dry so I took a sip from her bottle.

"This is not water; what is this?"

"Lemon drink-it gives me energy for work."

I took another sip. I liked it.

"This is really nice. Does your mother prepare it for you everyday?"

"No, I prepare it myself. My mother and father had divorced a year back. They are remarried to other people. Upon my graduation, they gave me a small house. I get to meet them occasionally. A maid does all the housework, but I like to cook for myself. I love cooking." She suddenly realised that she was talking non-stop.

"Sorry Sir, I just went on talking!"

"I also cook my food myself. I love cooking, although I can afford a cook." I showed no objection to her non-stop babbling.

"There is one more thing I want to tell you, Sir." I smiled and gave her a silent consent.

"Sir, you have very beautiful hair. I have longer hair but your hair is very silky and lovely. I dream to have such hair." I could not believe what she was saying. I was with a beautiful girl who had a perfect figure and a cute smile. And she was continuously praising me!

"We ladies in the office like your hair and wish to have hair like yours. Your hair looks so elegant; please don't cut them any shorter. I always wanted to tell you this but I was not sure how you will react considering your tough personality." People always like to praise their bosses. I did not take her seriously.

Fortunately, we reached her area and I hoped for some respite from this talkative lovely girl.

"Thank you again, Tapasya! Here is the Satadhar crossroad-now, which way to go?" She directed me to her home. I stopped the car in front of her home.

"I am thankful to you for the lift Sir!" She stood

outside the car window.

"You are always welcome!"

"Sir, if you don't mind, may I invite you inside for dinner?" She was excited to have dinner with her boss.

"I don't mind but I may not accept the invitation." Her face fell.

"Sir, it is almost eleven o'clock and you won't reach home before 11:30 pm. Don't you think it is a good idea to have dinner at my house?" I thought it was a great idea but something stopped me.

"Sir, I will never tell anybody that you had dinner with me, and I don't think I am a dangerous vamp." I realized how within a matter of minutes she has opened up to me. Her offer seemed irresistible.

She was right; she was not looking like a vamp. Actually, I was in no mood to go home and cook. I would have just eaten a sandwich. Every minute I was growing hungrier.

"Okay I will take you up on your offer but I have a condition. The condition is that I will help you in dinner preparation." She happily accepted the condition.

****

Chapter 8

We entered her well-kept beautifully decorated home. A large portrait of hers was hanging on a wall. Another wall had a painting showing bullocks tilling a farm. She owned a large 40-inch LED and a home theatre system. A two-by-three sized expensive looking sofa was arranged in the main hall artistically with a brownish black cover. The covers and curtains matched the colour of the wall.

"Sir, there is a guest room with wash room; you can use the wash room if you want to freshen up. I will just go change." It was a 2BHK house large enough for one person. The guestroom was also neat and clean. After freshening up in the bathroom I came out into the hall. I could see the kitchen on one side. Her kitchen was smaller than mine but looked more welcoming. After all, girls can take care of their house better.

She came out of her room. She had changed into jeans and T-shirt.

"So, what's on the menu?" I knew it was not possible to have an elaborate dinner.

"Whole grain spaghetti pasta with tomato sauce." She answered as she walked into the kitchen.

"Then let's start; my stomach is protesting loudly." I stood up and followed her.

She opened the fridge and brought out water and

one large sized apple.

"Sir, relax. It will not take more than ten minutes. But before that, drink the water and take this apple." She cut the apple in two halves, removed the core and offered me one of the halves. I was damn hungry, so I drank the water and took the apple.

Munching on the apple, she said, "Before cooking, I tie my hair in a ponytail. It is not a good idea to cook with hair loose. Sir, I think you should also tie your hair before we start cooking."

"No, I have never tied my hair. I like them free and loose."

"Sir, if you want to help me cook, you must tie your hair. This is my kitchen- I hope you don't mind." I finished my apple and noticed that she had already tied her hair in a ponytail.

"OK, I have no objection to following your kitchen rules only because I want to check out your cooking skills. But I don't have any skill or experience to tie my hair." I tried to wriggle out of her rules. On the other hand, I did not want to sit alone in the hall, among the piles of feminine items and fashion magazines.

"Leave it to me. If you allow, I can do it for you. It will not take more than a minute." She waited in anticipation.

"OK, no problem." Hearing my words she smiled

widely and rushed to her room.

"Keep your head still and look straight, Sir." She came back with a wide toothed comb and a headband.

She combed my hair from front to back, and then tugging them she tied them in a ponytail. I could feel the stretch in the hair roots. She had done a good job with the hair. But she was not done yet. She slipped a headband behind my ears, lowered it to my forehead and slid it to the crown of the head reining in some wayward hair falling.

"What is this?" I asked her, although I knew that it was a brown plastic toothed headband.

"It is a headband that will keep your hair away from your face. And now you are allowed to enter the kitchen." She did not break her promise-the comb over was done in just a minute.

She handed me a spare cooking apron. I was assigned to cut the vegetables, while she prepared the pasta. We finished cooking in just over ten minutes.

The whiff of the food spread in the kitchen and I felt even hungrier. I removed the apron, washed my hands, took a seat at the dinner table, and waited to be served the delicious dinner.

She also removed her apron and served the dinner in two plates. She brought cold drinks from the fridge and poured them into two glasses.

"You are a good cook!" I complimented her as I took another forkful of pasta.

"Thank you, Sir! It was all because of your help. You are not a bad cook yourself." She was quick to return the compliment.

A few moments passed in silence. She then served me a second helping. "I learned from my mother and also took some cooking classes. And where did you learn to cook, Sir?" She tried to make small talk.

"Some from my mother, some from friends and some from the internet."

"Girlfriend?" Her inner girl was coming out.

"No, I don't have a girlfriend." I was not lying.

"It is not possible. I can't believe that an intelligent and handsome looking man like you doesn't have a girlfriend." She continued her buttery language.

"I think you have lots of butter in your kitchen; that is why you have been continuously buttering me all evening."

"Sorry Sir, but I do not mean what you think."

"You are really a dream guy for city girls." She said the same thing that I have heard many times from other girls, relatives, friends, and even read it in magazines. This time, she was right: my name was on the top of the list of most eligible bachelors in the

Chapter 6

Work was meditation for me and the meditation was interrupted by Damajibhai who asked for permission to come to my office at 9:00 pm.

I checked the time. I was used to leaving the office at 10:00 pm and kept one key with me. Damajibhai, our head peon, usually left the office at 8:30 pm after everyone had left. His presence at this time surprised me.

"Damajibhai, why are you still here in the office?" I inquired.

"Sir, Tapasya madam is still working. I was waiting for her to leave." Damajibhai replied.

I never wanted my staff to be overburdened with the work and never encouraged them to stay late. I allowed Damajibhai to leave and asked him to instruct Miss Tapasya to leave too.

I finished work at 10:15 pm and put away my files. From the windows of the office, I could see that it was raining. The water drops came down gently on the window panes creating dreamy patterns. Rains always made me melancholic as I thought about life and losses.

I reined in my thoughts and slipped into a pair of casual brown 'Red Chief' leather shoes. I wrapped the platinum Rolex around my wrist. It was my rule never to carry any work or stress from office to home.

city.

"I think I am full." I stood up from the table carrying the empty plate to the kitchen.

She finished her meal also and carried the empty dishes to the kitchen. I dropped the plate into the basin and washed my hands. She gave me a napkin to wipe my hands.

I was feeling sleepy after the good meal and wanted to rush home but that would be bad manners so I sat down in the hall.

She cleaned the table and joined me with roasted salty aniseed in a small glass bottle in her hand.

I took two spoonfuls of aniseed.

"Thank you, Tapasya for the nice dinner." I stood up. "Now I should leave; it is already very late."

"I am obliged Sir, that you had dinner with me. And I am sorry if I said anything that hurt you. I could not stop talking with you around."

"No, none of your words hurt me. I enjoyed your company. OK, goodbye!" I started to walk to the door. I remembered that I had her hair accessories. I turned back and removed the headband from my hair and gave it to her.

"Sorry, forgot to return your headband and hairband."

"Keep that hair band."

"Thanks, but I don't tie my hair; and I don't think it will be of any use to me."

"But the ponytail looks great on you and this hairband is made of cloth material that will not hurt or break your hair."

"OK fine, thanks!" I did not want to waste time in discussion.

"Sir, wait a minute!" I had reached my car when she called me back. I turned back. She ran like a small child from her home to me and handed over my Rolex watch. I had removed it in the kitchen before cooking.

I thanked her again for the watch and dinner, and left for my home.

****

Chapter 9

Ahmad managed the party nicely. In addition to the dinner, he included dancing in the budget he was given.

The party was held in a banquet hall of 200-person capacity. Most of the staff members had already arrived with their families. They all eagerly introduced their family members to me. I could see the happiness on their faces as they shook my hand. Children of a few members touched my feet, a ritual I never liked and pleaded them not to do so. I requested everyone to enjoy the drinks and the party.

It was like any typical office get-together; wives of male members gossiped while the males themselves debated cricket, politics and company policies.

The company's future plan was a mystery to everyone. They tried to figure out what it was but they had no clue.

In some groups, men were busy flirting with the wives of others, and if lucky, with young beautiful ladies. Most of the males were attired in suits while females had more choices ranging from fancy dresses to traditional sarees.

I was standing near a wall mounted with one of the masterpieces of Dr. Ankur Zalawadia, a world famous painter from Gujarat.

Ahmad introduced me to his fiancée and parents.

I admired Ahmad's sincerity and knew he had a bright future ahead of him. After completion of the formalities, I asked them to enjoy the party. Mrs. Vrunda walked up to me with her family. After the introduction, I had a brief chat with her husband.

"Excuse me, please!" I saw Krunal entering the hall.

"Excuse me, Sir!" Tapasya shouted from the back. She was wearing an embroidered and stone work bodice and long sleeved pink net party dress that flaunted her curves. She had an elaborate hairdo and a seductive smile played on her face. Moderate makeup, smoky eyes, and dangling earrings made her look gorgeous.

For a moment, I was hypnotized by her look. I finally realized what I had been sensing all these years. I had liked her ever since the day when I interviewed her. Last night's interaction had reinforced those feelings. Suddenly, I realized that I was expecting some special guests to the party.

"Yes, Tapasya, you look gorgeous, and nice to see you! Enjoy the party; I will join you soon. I have some important work." She felt I was ignoring her and she looked clearly annoyed. I moved to Krunal who was accompanied by Mr. Mehta and his young daughter Kaumudi.

Mr. Mehta was the biggest name in the business world. He was also the richest man in India.

Mr. Mehta exuded class in his exclusive black suit. He was clean shaven with classically styled grey hair and wore a platinum chain around his neck.

I had invited Mr. Mehta to convince him to invest in my future plans of launching a female apparel brand. My reputation as a self-made businessman only enhanced his confidence in the new business.

He was to invest almost 300 crore rupees in the name of his 25 year old daughter, Kaumudi who had just completed her post-graduation in management from Harvard University.

Kaumudi was to join me as a partner in the company. Mr. Mehta wanted her to join his company but she had wanted to do something of her own. At about the same time, I had put a proposal to Mr. Mehta to invest in my future apparel foray. He liked the plan and asked Kaumudi to join me. She was also excited about the apparel industry, an industry her papa had not ventured into yet.

The father and daughter were in Ahmedabad that day for business. I grabbed my chance and invited them to meet my team.

"Good Evening, Mehta Sir! I am thankful you accepted my invitation to come to our small party."

"I am pleased to meet one of the promising businessmen. Prabuddh, meet my daughter, Kaumudi, and Kaumudi, this is…"

She was wearing a purple spaghetti top matched

with a light brown knee length skirt. From the skirt emerged shapely legs that seemed endless and were precariously balanced on three-inch-high heels.

Everything about Kaumudi was screaming class. Her large eyes looked amorous with thick eyelashes. An elegant retro hair style accentuated her oval face. The pink lips and a sexy mole on the neck left me stunned. I could not take my eyes off her. My pulse had quickened.

"This is Prabuddh. All management students know him; his success story '10 Lacs to 50 Crores' is taught in many institutes as a case study." Kaumudi seemed quite impressed by my success.

"Thank you Mr. Mehta, for the introduction!"

"Pleased to meet you, Madam." I brought out my million-dollar charismatic and enthralling rare smile. Any girl in this world would practically die to see that smile on my face.

"Please call me Kaumudi. After all, we are going to be business partners. And how may I call you?"

"Obviously, you can address me as Prabuddh, Kaumudi." I had already won half the battle. For me to fulfil my dream, a large investment and a well-known partner were important. More than the money, the association with Mehta was far more precious to my business. The Mehta association will help my new venture negotiate the government policies and help overcome other hurdles. Although there were about six months to official announcement and launch, a lot of work needed to be done.

"Sir, if you don't mind, may I announce your presence and introduce our business team to you?"

"Prabuddh, actually, I am in a hurry. I have to leave now."

"But Sir, dinner is ready." I tried to stop him so that I could impress him by showing off my business team.

"Prabuddh, I am already convinced to invest in your business, and now everything is up to Kaumudi. I have another business meeting that I have to attend. She will join you in the party. Please take care of her." He was in hurry; he was really a busy man.

His per-hour income was more than my monthly turnover, so the fifteen minutes he had spent with me cost him more than 100 crores, double of my annual turnover. Whatever he was planning to invest in my company was loose change for him. And so I didn't dare stop him.

Accompanied by Kaumudi, I went to the door to say goodbye to Mr. Mehta.

"Prabuddh, please don't announce my presence here. Actually, I hate formalities." Kaumudi requested, as we made our way back to the party.

"Sir, the dinner is served. Should we start?" Ahmad asked.

"Ahmad, the whole plan is yours; there is no need to ask for any permission."

"Sir, as I had informed you yesterday, a dance hour is arranged after dinner."

"Ahmad, you are allowed to rock the floor after dinner with your fiancée."

"Kaumudi, he is Ahmad, the talented and enthusiastic new Marketing Head of Ahmedabad branch."

"Hi, I am Kaumudi-nice to meet you, Mr. Ahmad!" She shook hands with Ahmad.

"I am also pleased to meet you Miss Kaumudi." Ahmad, unaware of his future boss, muttered.

"Ahmad, please announce the dinner."

"Kaumudi, what will you like to have?" As Ahmad was announcing the dinner, I asked the beautiful lady to accompany me.

"I will have some pineapple juice."

"Waiter, one pineapple juice for the lovely lady and an orange juice for me."

The waiter appeared with orange juice that had lemon tucked to rim of the glass and pineapple juice with straw and lemon on the edge.

"I have read and heard many things about you and your work attitude, Prabuddh." I was not sure what she was getting to.

"I hope they were all good!" I tried to have some fun."

"You should know that the fashion magazines notice your fashion style and hairstyle. Your hair looks quite sexy. Girls are crazy about your hair. I am going to hate you if you cut your hair." I blushed. I could not understand what was going on! First Tapasya and now Kaumudi – girls were going crazy about me and my hair!

"Good Evening Sir! Should I bring you your dinner?" Tapasya appeared out of nowhere. She might have overheard Kaumudi.

"Kaumudi, please meet Miss Tapasya, our director of our new branch in Surat. And Tapasya, this is Kaumudi."

"New friend of Prabuddh? Pleased to meet you." Both cats air kissed each other.

Temperatures soared. I could swear I smelled something burning!

"Pleased to meet you too." Tapasya replied with a charming smile. She was jealous alright.

"Nice dress, Tapasya! Who is the designer?"

"I designed it myself. Fashion designing is my hobby."

"Oh, great! Will you design one for me?"

"You are already wearing one from the collection

of Manish Arora-one of the best designers in India. It looks very attractive on your figure."

They started with the fashion industry, and then discussed jewellery. Sometime later the conversation reached hair styling, makeup and shoes.

Gradually, the initial jealousy was replaced by girl talk and lots of giggling. They forgot my presence.

"OK ladies, you can continue your girl talk. Tapasya, will you please take care of Kaumudi?"

"Sure Sir; if Kaumudi does not mind."

"I don't mind; Tapasya is quite good company."

I did not like the way both ladies ignored my presence. Now it was my turn to be jealous.

"Do you have anything important to discuss, Prabuddh?" Kaumudi stopped me.

"No, nothing, except having dinner; and both of you look like old friends."

"Then let us have dinner together. I am also hungry."

****

Chapter 10

After the party got over, I dropped Kaumudi off at her Marriott Hotel. Her company was entertaining; she was more free minded in comparison to Tapasya. She had a lively nature, and she spoke on variety of topics in addition to the happenings in the business world. Kaumudi was not only beautiful but also seemed intelligent. I was excited to be partnering with her. In the short ride to hotel, she had impressed me with her creative ideas and thoughts.

"If everything goes right, nobody will be able to stop me.' I thought as I waved at her.

I had arranged a meeting with her at her hotel the next evening at 8:00 pm to discuss the new project.

I had taken a lot of time to prepare the presentation and discussed it with my best subordinates. Everything had to be perfect. The meeting was very important to me; all my dreams depended on the meeting and the presentation.

Initially, I thought I would dress formally but I wanted to convey the real me; the confident young swashbuckling tycoon. I chose the casual look. My presentation explained the business plan for the first five years that included investment needed, balance sheets, cash flows, entry strategy and marketing. The father and daughter were impressed with the roadmap of the new business. They were sold to my plan.

Kaumudi confirmed her partnership in the project and wanted the venture to start as early as possible. For her father the investment was a minor matter but for me it was very important.

We signed the partnership agreement. I was waiting for the money to come in. The blueprint of the business was already prepared. I was all set to embark on the journey of 1000 crore rupees project.

Mr. Mehta was to leave for Delhi. The project required Kaumudi to stay in Ahmedabad for almost a week. She wanted to start work on the project as soon as possible which was fine with me. The situation demanded that I fix a meeting with the research team to decide next plan of action. Up until that time the project was not disclosed to anybody in the office, except to the research and finance heads of department. I had worked a lot on the plan while Tapasya too had a part to work on. It was important that Tapasya too would understand the urgency and finished the work immediately. I wanted to call and remind her but I trusted her and knew she would not fail me.

****

Chapter 11

Next morning, as usual, I was the first to arrive in office. I took a few moments to meditate and to pray to God and to my parents. I had just opened my project file when there was a knock on my door.

"May I come in, Sir?" Tapasya had apparently come early today. She must have rushed directly to my office before going to her cabin.

"Please come in."

"Sir, the file you wanted is complete." Tapasya informed me. I gave a sigh of relief because the plan was to be discussed with Kaumudi that evening.

"Good, Tapasya you are a woman of your words. Let me go through the file, I will call you later if required."

I went through the file; she had done better than my expectations. While reading the file, an idea flickered in my brain. I worked rapidly on the thought and did some calculations while making the necessary changes in the file.

Damajibhai brought tea for me. I walked to the window with tea in my hand. Something was bothering me. I again ran the idea through my mind. I had some lingering doubts. Should I do that? Why am I doing that? Was it because of feelings for her in my heart? Was I distracted from my aim?

Answers were hard to come by. All I knew was

that the idea was profitable for me. I decided to call Tapasya in my office.

She appeared in no time even as I was figuring out what to say to her. I signalled her to sit.

"Tapasya, after going through your file, I have decided something for you."

She continued to purse her lips. After a pause, I said, "I am sure you would have understood the purpose of the file you prepared, but still I will brief you about it."

"Yes Sir!"

"We are going to launch a new wing of our company in the form of female garments in partnership with the Mehta Group. Kaumudi, Mr. Mehta's daughter, is partnering with us. They are investing 300 crores and our company is investing about 700 crores for a 1000 crore rupees project. Before we recruit a few more employees for the company, I want you to assist in the project."

"Seems interesting, and I will be happy to assist, but Sir, I have a question. In the whole story, I could not understand where the 700 crores will come from."

"That can be disclosed to you only after you confirm the proposal. Your role will be as director. Salary and perks will be the same. But yes you will have to travel extensively to Delhi, Ahmedabad, and

Mumbai frequently from Surat."

"Does that mean I will have to continue with the Surat branch?"

"Yes, you will remain and work as director of the Surat branch for an initial two to three month period. As the branch becomes stable, we will announce our new foray, and you will be the full time director of the new extension."

"This does seem interesting and I will like to take on the added responsibility. This also means that you are going to double my responsibility." I noticed the change in her. This was the professional Tapasya speaking.

"No, I am giving you a chance to become a partner in my company. You will get 1% shares of the new company upon official registration. That will amount to about 10 crore rupees on its basic rate, though its market price could be much higher." I revealed the actual benefit she was to get by the added responsibility. I had taken a big decision without consulting with Kaumudi first.

"It is a very attractive offer and I accept it. But my question remains the same–where will the 700 crores come from?" The glee in her eyes was not from her financial benefit but came from something else and that something. I knew and it was called love.

"I will mortgage this company and my home to the bank for a loan of 700 crores. All paperwork has been completed; money will come in instalments from the bank as the project progresses."

"Sir, you are taking quite a big financial risk." I was confused whether she was concerned or simply warning against the risk I was taking!

"No, I don't think so. You must have noticed in your file that after the launch of the product we will recover the whole cost of the project within a year."

I did not tell her that I was going to recover my money from the IPO of my existing company, for which I would have to improve the financial sheet of the company.

****

Chapter 12

We all worked hard for several months, assisted by my entire team. We already had textile supply coming from the Ahmedabad branch. Surat branch was all set to supply other varieties of the textiles. The Head Office of the new company was to be established in Ahmedabad, while the branches were to be setup in Mumbai, Delhi, and Bangalore, to cover the entire country.

For the vigorous launch of the company and brand, we needed to hire fashion designers, tailors, and for few more positions.

We took over three local apparel factories in Ahmedabad to manufacture the female clothes. Their employees would undergo training of two to three days for the new designs and stitching.

Finance flow was not disturbed and everything was going as planned. We did some great piece of work.

On the other hand, I had frequent business trips to Delhi and Mumbai; either Ahmad or Tapasya accompanied me in most them.

I knew Tapasya better as I came closer to her, she was more of cheerful nature than I guessed for her. she was skilled to find out happiness from little things. She was fond of taking selfies and had lots of selfies with me at airport, restaurants and everywhere she got the chance.

We had many occasion to get outside and had had food in restaurants. She was successful to make me see movie with her in multiplex even after hectic schedule.

We both knew each other's likes and dislikes. She cared my every need that made me dependant on her gradually.

Our body language had expressed love many times but those three magic words were never exchanged.

****

Chapter 13

Once in a Delhi ....

We were interviewing candidates for the positions of Marketing Officer, Accountant, and Branch Manager for the Delhi branch. It was very busy day in Delhi and we were mentally tired. Kaumudi forced me and Tapasya to stay for the night at her home. We accepted her proposal and postponed our flight to the next morning.

Kaumudi, by now, had also become a good friend. Although I was a business partner and friend to Kaumudi, Tapasya was closer to her. That might be the reason why Kaumudi invited us to stay in her home.

A large, oval-shaped dinner table was filled with more than 50 varieties of Thai, Chinese, Italian and German dishes. I had not heard the names of most of the dishes.

Mr. Mehta was out of town and could not join us in the dinner, but Mrs. Mehta gratified us by accompanying us to the dinner.

After dinner, Kaumudi proposed a walk outside. Her bungalow had a large garden decorated with every conceivable flower plant. A coffee table with four chairs was placed in the centre of the garden near a rubber tree. On one side of the garden was a swimming pool and the other side had tennis and basketball courts.

After the walk around the garden we sat around the coffee table. Kaumudi had her favourite pink roses in her hand. We all were in a light mood and the girls had already started gossiping and discussing hairstyles. I was getting bored by such talk and started playing with my new Samsung 6 Edge Plus mobile.

"Tapasya, what do you think about Prabuddh's hairstyle? He would look great in a ponytail." Kaumudi had already noticed me surfing the mobile and tried to drag me into their discussion.

"Of course, he looks great in a ponytail." Tapasya was also big mouth like any other girl.

"That means he has tried a ponytail and I have never seen him in one." Kaumudi got the message.

I frowned at Tapasya; I did not want others gossiping about my hair style. Tapasya was not to be intimidated easily.

"Sorry girls, I am sleepy. You both enjoy your gossiping." I got up.

"Prabuddh let us tie your hair into a ponytail and only then you will be allowed to sleep." Kaumudi pleaded.

"Kaumudi, you are so like a little girl."

"Please… please… please…." both girls squealed in a chorus.

I had no other option but to give in.

Tapasya stood up and picked the comb out of her purse; she knew that I did not know how to tie a ponytail.

"Tapasya, if you don't mind, let me try this time." Kaumudi was trying to have fun. I felt that I was like a Barbie doll to them.

Kaumudi brushed my hair and collected them into her fist. She had a pink hair band in her purse while Tapasya had one with bright red butterflies. Kaumudi loosened a few strands of my hair making them rest on my face.

Both girls enjoyed the Barbie doll game with my hair, trying out different types of hair styles for about half an hour, turn by turn. I had to bear their games because I wanted to become the richest man in the world and both these girls were the key to fulfilling my dream. Finally, they approved a half ponytail for my hair, tied by the red butterfly hairband with rest of the hair free.

I noticed both the girls had the same hairstyle, they did not miss the chance to take pics.

Both pleaded with me to keep my hair tied for the night. I had no choice but to entertain them.

****

Chapter 14

I was given a separate bedroom, and after leaving the girls, I went to my bedroom.

The large bedroom had a king-sized double bed covered with a soft-bluish bed cover. Two split ACs were chilling the room. One side of the bedroom had a bookshelf full of books and magazines while the other side had a full size mirror.

I removed my clothes and went into the washroom to shower. A fluffy blue towel was hanging in the bathroom which I draped around my waist and came out of the bathroom. I stepped towards my night dress.

I could see myself in the mirror. Even with a demanding schedule, I always worked out every morning and the result was there to see–a muscular body with a six-pack abdomen. I liked what I saw. It was time to put on my sleeping clothes.

As I turned around, I was startled to see Tapasya standing at the bedroom door.

"When did you come?" I was not sure if she saw me dressing up.

"I came when you were in the shower. You have such a masculine body and that six-pack is such a turn-on."

"Why are you here?"

"I am here to take my butterfly back."

"I do not remember where I threw that girlish thing."

"I only had one and will need it tomorrow."

"Oh alright! It will be somewhere here; let me find it. Why don't you look on the other side of the bed?"

We started our search operation. We saw the butterfly lying on the bed. We both jumped reflexively on the bed at the same time and butted our heads. She yelled in pain.

I apologized to her as I held her head in my hands. She was staring into my eyes with her deep dark eyes. I could smell her fruity breath on my face. Without makeup her face looked fresh. I noticed that her luscious lips were naturally pink. Pulled in by an irresistible urge I kissed her on her mouth. She reciprocated by sliding her tongue in my mouth. Her fruity breath and lingering taste of her strawberry flavoured lip gloss combined to singe my senses. We both sank to the bed holding each other tightly.

****

Chapter 15

She was sleeping when I came back to the bedroom at 6:00 am after finishing my morning workout. I did not disturb her and went to shower. She was sitting in the bed when I came out of the bathroom with the towel around my waist.

"Hi! Good Morning!" I was not sure how to start the conversation.

"Good Morning!"

"I am sorry about last night... if... but..." I stammered.

"It's OK!"

"You should get ready; we have a flight to catch to Mumbai."

"If you don't mind, may I use your bathroom?"

"Sure."

She got out of the bed and pulled the towel off me and ran into the bathroom playfully. I did not expect that.

"Hey, my towel! I gave permission for the bathroom only."

She opened the bathroom door and threw her lingerie at me.

I dressed into casual clothes and packed my luggage. She was still in the bathroom.

Kaumudi came into the room after knocking on the door.

"Hey, Prabuddh, come down for breakfast. I can't find Tapasya in her room, have you seen her?"

Before I could answer, Tapasya came out of the bathroom with the towel around her chest.

Kaumudi's eyes widened with surprise. "Oh, looks like both of you had a great time last night." She noticed the lingerie lying around.

"We will come down for breakfast as soon as Tapasya is ready." I gave that look to Tapasya.

"What?" Tapasya reacted.

"Nothing! Get ready. We have to catch a flight."

She changed into the clothes from last night in my presence and went to her room.

"Wait, I'll just get ready and pack the luggage and then we will go down together."

She came back within twenty minutes wearing a pink shirt and skin tight beige jeans. She looked stunning with her hair loose. She matched her outfit with pink dangling earrings. She had no makeup except mascara and pink lipstick.

Her milky white cheeks looked adorable with the dimples when she smiled. "I am not going to use this; you can take it."

She gave me her butterfly hairband without even waiting for my reply. Like she did last night, she combed my long hair and tied it into a half ponytail with the help of the butterfly hairband.

"Tapasya, I am not sure how to say this. I will not be able to marry you in the near future even though you are a good girl and I like you very much because…"

"Because your business is your priority. I know you will not marry till you achieve your goal."

"Prabuddh, I want to hear what any girl will die to hear from you."

I turned back, held her by shoulders, looked into her eyes and said, "I love you Tapasya."

I did say those words but knew the words did not come from my heart. I was still in a dilemma.

We had enjoyed each other's bodies making love last night. Tapasya had it all what a guy wanted in a girl. She was smart and looked fantastic. But all I had on my mind was my business and money. There was no place in my heart for a girlfriend. I was just a guy who wanted to make more money.

"I love you too, and also trust you Prabuddh. And now you are reserved for me only. I have put my stamp on you."

"Where is the stamp?"

"In your hair-my butterfly! From now on you will regularly wear your hair in a ponytail tied by my butterfly. And that is my stamp on you."

"Let us have our breakfast." I smiled and kissed her lips.

****

Chapter 16

My core company performed very well in next six months. The audited financial sheet showed a growth of 400% in sales and 370% growth in profit. It was an excellent performance by both our branches. The market value of the company zoomed to more than 2000 crore rupees with each share valued at one lakh rupees.

I was on the cover page of most of the business magazines. It was miraculous that the company value had increased twenty times in just six months. My efficient financial team had worked hard to keep the books clean to satisfy the income tax department and government.

We announced the new brand of female apparel in the market as a new subsidiary in association with Mehta Group. The marketing team had already spread the news of the impending launch. The business world was agog for the official announcement.

'Ponytail' was the name suggested by Tapasya for the new brand. The name was approved by Kaumudi and the marketing team. The campaign blitz of 100 crore rupees was ready to be unleashed. Our fashion designers had created the complete range of female fashion wear. The more than 100 designs were exhibited at the Mumbai branch at the time of official announcement.

Our research team had worked meticulously and our manufacturing department working in tandem with the technology department was successful in keeping the manufacturing costs lowest in the industry. We supplied low cost clothes of the best quality. Our label filled a long unfulfilled gap in the female fashion wear market.

We received orders of 300 crore rupees in just two days of launch from the wholesalers and retail chains. The orders were fulfilled in just a week.

I grabbed the chance and launched IPO of my parent company and offered 30% of the company to the public. The IPO was oversubscribed by 40 times. I had offered 10 rupee share at 990 rupees which was listed at a premium of 30%. I collected 1300 crore rupees by selling 13 million shares of my parent company. With the IPO turning into a huge success my horizons expanded even further. I was able to clear my debt and had a few more crore rupees in hand to expand. Prajwalit Ltd continued its expansion spree and now our footprint expanded to 10 branches and 25 manufacturing units all over India. The Research Team was ordered to study the global market for our label.

'Ponytail' creative team was successful in designing a new line of clothes for every season. Our market strategy was simple: keep profit margins higher for the bestselling latest apparel lines. We worked hard and we celebrated our success at every step. The market value of 'Ponytail' hit 5000 crore rupees in short time. It was time to eye the male apparel market.

We soon launched the new series of male apparel and created a chain of 300 franchises selling 'Ponytail' branded apparel. Quality, design, styles and innovation kept growing the 'Ponytail' brand and with it my hunger of money. 'Ponytail' promoters were Tapasya, Kaumudi, and me. I was the biggest stock holder with 60% share, Kaumudi's share was 30% and Tapasya held 5% share. Another 5% share was held by various politicians and other sundry people.

****

Chapter 17

"What is next?" Kaumudi questioned. We all three were enjoying lunch at the Taj Hotel in Mumbai after a meeting with the branch managers of 'Ponytail'.

"I have eyes on the software business and I'm planning to hire a consulting firm to give me a business plan for the global business of medical software." I replied with my eyes on the plate and hands playing with the food.

"I was just wondering what the next big thing is for 'Ponytail'?" Kaumudi clarified her query.

Just then, a group of teenagers entered the restaurant. Everyone had funky hair styles and funky clothes. We noticed that not a single girl or boy was wearing clothing from 'Ponytail' brand. We discerned a unisex variety of clothes. A few boys had girlish T-shirts and trousers while two of the girls wore masculine clothes.

We three observed the group. They were from rich families and had enough disposable money to spend on clothes.

We came back to our discussion.

"Are you both thinking what I am thinking?" Tapasya asked.

"Yes, a line of clothes for the new generation,

including unisex clothes." Kaumudi nodded.

"In other words, girlish clothes for boys and boyish style for girls." I cleared the concept.

"And that will increase Ponytail's business like Prabuddh's growing ponytail." Both girls giggled.

I hated their discussion every time about my long hairs. I noticed that my hair was longer than either of the girls and almost reached halfway down my back. Both girls regularly visited salons to get their hair cut and styled. I always avoided the barber because of my greed and busy business schedule.

"Don't harass him; he is my little princess and I like to make his ponytail." Tapasya's comment made both girls giggle again and me humiliated.

"We cannot launch the unisex apparel line as our main business or on a large scale. We will have to first sensitize our customers to the changing fashion trends." I was already thinking ahead.

We decided to give the idea a chance and with it a budget of 50 crores for the research, design and launch of the product. The 'Ponytail' team had a new challenge.

****

Chapter 18

We could see the dark sky with twinkling stars and full moon from the garden terrace of my bungalow. I and Tapasya were relishing the cool environment on a summer night after frenetic schedule of the week. It was a Saturday night and Tapasya was oiling her hair. I was listening to old melodious songs lying on a reclining chair.

"Tapasya" I broke the silence.

"Hmm..." she continued to massage her hair.

"If a situation is created in which I have to ..." I opened my eyes trying to search for appropriate words. She continued to pamper her hair.

"If there is situation where you need to leave me, what will you do?" I could sense her fingers had stopped caressing her hair.

"You should take rest from the work. All this work is creating such thoughts in your head." She did not take my question seriously and this time started oiling my hair.

"I am not kidding."

"I will never leave you, whatever may be the situation." I was feeling relaxed by her massage on my head. The lilting music spun magic in the background.

"I was thinking we should marry." I surprised her when she was making bun on my head. I waited for her answer. She slipped her arms around my neck and caressed my chest with her long fingers.

"Are you really ready for marriage?" she asked.

"I have achieved enough and there are still many more things left to achieve. I need you as life partner in my future journey." I dropped myself in her lap. Her face hid the full moon behind and the glow of the moon appeared around her face like a halo. She was still caressing my chest when her fingers paused for a second.

Her smiling face turned into a serious expression, "Prabuddh, I can't live without you; even if you have thought about another girl but you will never lose me." I knew she was really serious and meant what she said. She was perfect for the future plan I had in my mind. I kept looking at her face but could not make contact with her eyes. I got up.

"See the moon is hiding behind the clouds but still its glow is visible!" I drew her attention to the sky.

As she looked up to see the moon, I grabbed my chance and brought out the engagement ring. She did not notice my slow little movement and kept looking at the moon.

When she looked at me she was shocked and surprised. She saw me kneeling before her and holding the engagement ring.

"Tapasya, will you be my life partner?" I was proposing to the girl, although I knew her answer.

"No!" I almost lost my balance, shocked by her answer.

"First tell me the magic words." She was really a romantic girl at heart after all.

I stood up, and whispered in her ear as the melodies played out.

"Tapasya, hu tane khara hridaythi prem karu chu. Su tu mari sathe lagn karis?"

(Tapasya, I love you by heart. Will you marry me?)

She hugged me, and put her head on my chest. "I will marry you and will spend my whole life with you." We stood there embracing each other. I realized her tears had wet my shirt.

"Tapasya, why are you crying? These eyes are not made to cry." I wiped her tears.

"These tears are of happiness, let them flow. I was waiting for this chance to cry all these years."

I could not say anything. My eyes were on her beautiful face. I kissed her everywhere-on her eyes, on her cheeks, on her lips, feeling her warmth on my face. It was the most beautiful and memorable night for me. I had taken one more step towards my goal.

****

Chapter 19

There were lots of things happening in my life. We planned to marry next month. On the business side, I wanted to launch a new venture in medical software. I called in a meeting of the parent company; Prajwalit Ltd. Tapasya was no longer in the parent company. Now she was full time director in 'Ponytail'.

I put the idea of venturing into Medical Software to the team and received mixed reactions. Some team members thought that the idea was risky since we did not have any core competence in that sector. I could sense that the team was not too gung-ho about the new project. I would have to think about it a little more.

I came out of my Ahmedabad branch office and powered the engine of my brand new silver 1.5L BMW i8.

It was a winter evening in Ahmedabad and the sun was sinking in the horizon. The sky was a fiery orange. The clouds changed colours every few minutes. Below it was rush hour on the roads. I drove to the riverfront, parked the car, got out and started to walk. People were enjoying one of the few winter evenings dressed in their woollens and jackets. I sat on an empty bench facing the river.

A few elders and some young couples were roaming along the riverfront. Two senior citizens passed by me jogging slowly. The riverfront was quiet cold and I was just wearing a casual half sleeve T-shirt. I was getting cold, so I rubbed my hands and put them on my face and closed my eyes.

A few years earlier, the Sabarmati was a foul smelling river with slums all around. It wasn't pleasant to come here. Few years later, the riverfront had developed into a happening and beautiful place with people spending their evenings and holding picnics here.

Few steps away a homeless man was lying on the pavement with no clothes on. His bed was made up of a plastic advertisement banner. I recognized the banner; it was from the promotion of 'Ponytail Male New Collection!' The man shivered in the cold.

He tried to cover his body with the banner. A chill ran through my spine–not from the cold but from watching this withered body lying naked in this cold.

I could not watch this anymore. I got up, and removed my blue 'Ponytail' T-shirt. The chilly wind made me shiver and I thought I might catch a cold.

The sun had set turning the orange skies dark. I walked up to the man and touched his body; he did not move. I tried once more, but again, he did not respond. Perhaps the cold weather had made him unconscious. I again tried to wake the man. This time he moved and looked weakly into my eyes. I gave him my T-shirt. He could not understand what I

was trying to do.

"Take this and oblige me."

He took the T-shirt, even though it would not offer much warmth but it might give him some protection. I walked away without caring what he was going to do with the T-shirt.

I had parked the car a kilometre away. I started to run to warm my body. A few young collegian girls were having fun on the riverfront and I could sense them checking out my muscular body with my long hair thrashing my back. They passed a comment. They might have thought I was some sort of perverted or crazy middle aged man running around with no shirt on this chilly evening.

The running had warmed my body. I was perspiring and my vest was wet. I got to my car, but decided to take another round passing the girls again. This time my whole body was wet with perspiration, the vest was glued to my body and my muscles; my long hair glistened with beads of sweat. My chest pumped like an engine. My breathing was rapid and warm; I was not feeling cold anymore. This time the girls did not laugh-this time their eyes widened and their mouths literally drooled ogling at my rippling muscles. I noticed their expression with amusement. I came back to my car. The run made me feel good though a little tired. I reached in the trouser pocket for the car keys.

"Hey, Prabuddh!" a hand patted my back and I

heard a feminine voice.

"Oh Mahek-nice to see you again after so many years!" I recognized the girl who had a crush on me during my college days. She had proposed to a rude and selfish man like me and in return got hurt by me. She had wanted to marry me.

"It seems you have been working out! You are looking more handsome than you did in college. She could not take her eyes away from me and I could not resist her words.

"And longer hair too!" I taunted her.

"Yes, but now, it does not matter to me. What are you doing here? You are very rich and famous nowadays. And your 'Ponytail' is a learning lesson for new industrialists!" she started the conversation.

"I came here to take a break from the work. How about you?"

"I am here with my husband to celebrate Diwali holidays in Ahmedabad. My husband is a programmer in an IT company in Hyderabad and I work as a software developer in the same company."

A bald man appearing more aged than myself, with a bulging belly and a loose XXXL sized T- shirt on his flabby body, walked up to Mahek. She had also collected a fair amount of fat on her face and body, but she was still looking beautiful enough.

"Hi Agnesh! Meet the 'Businessman of the Year',

Prabuddh. Prabuddh, this is Agnesh my husband." We shook hands. He looked surprised to see me without a shirt.

"Nice to meet you! All the jogging made me perspire a lot, so I removed the T-shirt."

With the formal introduction over, I got to know that he was a software professional of a top IT company in the country. An idea took root in my mind and I invited them to dinner. They had planned to eat out so they accepted my invitation. The venue was the Fortune landmark on Ashram Road. I excused myself for half an hour to change my clothes. Tapasya was out of the city and was to come back late night.

I phoned my team to find out the position and influence of Mahek and her husband in their company. They got back to me just before dinner confirming that they had influential positions in their company.

At the restaurant while coming out of the wash room, I realized I had lost my hairband. Mahek had an extra one of green colour that she offered to me. She tied my long hair with it.

We enjoyed the dinner, recalling the crazy moments of college life. Then, we discussed Mahek's and her husband Agnesh's professional work. I conveyed a strong message that I had eyes on medical software development. Agnesh was quite intelligent and understood what I was getting at and the real motive of inviting them to the dinner. He stood up and excused himself.

He returned soon and announced that he had fixed my meeting with the chairman of his company. I was impressed with his quick thinking and decisiveness.

Agnesh's company had not diversified much and therefore wanted to expand its business. They needed an investor. I had no experience in the field and no knowledge, but had the money to invest in the company. The meeting was fixed for two days later in Bangalore. We waved and parted. I again ordered my subordinates to carry out due diligence of the company including its financial position and report back to me within two days.

****

Chapter 20

I returned home and opened the door. Tapasya was sitting in the main hall watching television. She would drop in whenever she was in Ahmedabad. It was almost 11:00 pm.

Her face was contorted with anger. I got some water from the fridge and went over to her.

Sometimes, she played with emotions and created drama, just to take the attention off me, so I did not think much of it.

"Darling, I have some good news." I pressed her shoulders from behind eager to tell her about the meeting.

"And I have bad news for you."

"Ok, what is it? Let us start with the bad news first."

She jerked her shoulders to brush away my hands. I was surprised by her act. She stood up and threw some photographs from her purse at me.

The photographs were of me and Mahek, talking near my car. I did not have a shirt on and the photographs were taken from such an angle that it looked like I was kissing Mahek. I was stunned by the pictures.

Before I could say anything, she started crying even as tears rolled down from her eyes. She told me to turn around. When I did, she pulled the hairband from my hair and asked where it came from.

"It is… Honey, let me explain."

She again handed me a photograph, this time showing Mahek tying my hair with her hairband. Once again, the photographer was tricky enough not to show Agnesh.

"Darling, let me explain."

"I trusted you. You are just like the other men. I never believed it when people told me about your colourful life. But how can I not believe these photographs? Aren't these photos yours?"

"These photos are mine, but it is not what you think. Mahek was my college friend and I just ran into her today after all these years."

"And you kissed her, had dinner with her, and let her replace my stamp from your ponytail."

"Give me a chance to explain."

"I know that you are clever and you will convince me that the photographer had used tricks. You have hurt me and have broken my heart."

I tried to explain everything to her but she did not believe me and kept crying.

"And what reason will you give for this lipstick stain on your shirt?"

It was just a lipstick stain, not even lip marks, and I did not know where it came from.

"I don't know where the stain came from." I replied honestly.

"I am getting out of your life and your home. Now, never try to talk to me without having a strictly professional reason. I don't want to share any future dreams with you anymore."

Before I could stop her, she left the home. I tried to call her but could not reach her. The next evening, a local police inspector called me to identify a dead body they had found floating on the river front.

The body was decomposed but it was unmistakably her–the tight ponytail and large eyes. The face was swollen and blue as if she was still angry with me. Her eyes still seemed to be crying. It seemed she had drunk lots of water to cool her anger down.

****

A year has passed since I last saw her. She had left this home and left me. Her death had broken me. I lost my parents when I had no money. And then I lost Tapasya even when I had lots of money.

I understood the game of God. He first gives you everything then takes away who you care about. I now understood what it is like to not care about people. We understand their true worth only when we lose them.

I withdrew from my business and now 'Ponytail' is fully owned by Kaumudi. I sold her my shares and in turn got lots of money in my bank account to last me my entire life.

Now I spent my days at my home. In the mornings I cooked food with my ponytail tied and then later in the day wrote stories with my hair tied in bun like Tapasya used to do. I had stopped working out. I stayed inside my home all day and looked depressed. I was eating fatty stuff all day and looked like a pig. I neither met anyone nor gave appointments to anyone.

****

Section 2

Ponytail: The Love for Revenge

One year after the death of Tapasya...

One morning, I allowed Ahmad to come meet me along with his wife. He had been running the company on my behalf. I got part of the profit. He believed that one day I will be back to running the company and Prajwalit Ltd will be restored to its old glory.

The doorbell rung and he came in with his wife. His wife went to the kitchen and brought water for all of us.

Ahmad put a file on the table. He asked me to go through the file but I did not show any interest.

After he left, I saw a photo of three ponytails taken at Kaumudi's house sticking out of the file. I picked the photo and recalled the photographer of this 'Three Ponytails' photo. The photographer had a professional camera and he was wearing black party shoes.

There were other photos in the file. There was the surreptitiously taken photo of me and Mahek at the

Sabarmati riverfront. In the car side view mirror, I could see the reflection of the same photographer who had taken the 'Three Ponytails' photo.

I got off the sofa and grabbed the phone and thanked Ahmad and announced, "I am coming back to the business."

Chapter 21

I got up and walked to the mirror. I hadn't shaved for some days. My face did not glow like it did a year ago; eyes were swollen red while the cheeks were puffed up with layers of fat. My belly stretched the T-shirt and my muscles had lost their tone. My hair was still long but had lost their luster.

I walked to my Renault Duster. This was the car that had brought me and Tapasya close. I slid my hand over the passenger seat. Tapasya had sat here as she laughed, teased me about my hair, pampered me and invited me for dinner.

"Sir, the media is waiting. We should leave now." Ahmad interrupted my thoughts.

"Let's go." I sat in Ahmad's black Mercedes Benz.

"Nice car, Ahmad!"

"I am thankful to you Sir that I am able to afford this car."

"You have succeeded because of your hard work and dedication. Anyway, how is Surabhi?"

"She is fine; she is also excited that you are coming back to Prajwalit."

"Ahmad, yes, I am coming back but not back to Prajwalit!" Ahmad suddenly stopped the car with the brakes screeching. He was shocked by what he just heard.

"Are you going to start a new company?"

"No! Actually I am going to join Ponytail!"

"And this press conference is for…" He trailed off. He was still confused. We stood in the middle of the road. He ignored the blaring horns.

"First of all start the car!" He followed my order. The silence between us was uncomfortable.

"Ahmad, I am not going to appear in the press conference. I am going to the airport now." I tried to make sense of things for him He turned the car towards the airport. He could not comprehend what was going on. He continued to listen.

"You will announce that you have thrown me out of the company." I said.

"Why? Media will ask me why I had done so."

"Just say that I sold you my entire share in the company."

"And then?"

"In addition announce that I sold my home and everything to you to pay my debts."

"Will media believe that?"

"I don't know, but they love such headlines and will publicize it." I paused, closed my eyes and pushed back my seat.

Ahmad was driving but he was more interested in my plan. He knew if he announced something like this the share prices of Prajwalit Ltd would take a big hit. The stock had been stable for some time since I continued to be in the Board of Directors; though the stock had not appreciated from the time of handing over the management to Ahmad. He was good manager but did not have the vital entrepreneur instincts that I had.

"For now drop me at the Airport. I have a Delhi flight in an hour."

"Delhi?"

"Yes."

"Sir, but if I announce what you just said, then…"

"Then?"

"The stock will tank."

"I know it will crash; but not for long time. The company will continue to perform. The stock will rise again."

We were at the 'Departure' area of the airport. I got out with my bag.

He looked concerned.

"Sir, whatever you do, please be careful!"

"Don't worry. I have lost enough. And losing money does not scare me." I started to walk towards the entry gate.

"Ahmad, see you soon!" I turned around and waved at him smiling. His face twinkled.

I entered the airport just as they were announcing the departure of my flight.

****

Chapter 22

"Welcome Sir, happy to see you after a long time!" One of airhostess greeted me smiling artificially. I had no idea how she recognized me.

"Thanks Amita, nice to see you too." She had a name tag on her shirt.

I used to be a frequent flyer and was quite famous because of my ponytail. Most flight attendants knew me. But my looks have changed and I looked like a different person.

Then I remembered. Amita had once asked for my autograph on her hanky. We once met after her duty hours. She was one of my genuine fans and would message me frequently and I would reply to her occasionally. She escorted me to my seat.

"You have put on weight Sir." She was a little hesitant. "I would not have recognized you if I had not read your name on the boarding pass."

"Hopefully you might not need to read when we meet again." I joked.

"I would like to see your old self again." She smiled and walked away. She had to attend to other passengers.

I put on the safety belt and promptly fell asleep.

"Sir, will you like to have vegetarian or non-vegetarian breakfast?" I was ready to show my exasperation for disturbing my sleep when I noticed her sharp cheek bones and bluish large beautiful eyes. She had gathered her hair in tight bun. It was apparent from the size of bun that she had much longer hair. She had a nice Indian figure, quite different from the usual zero figure flight airhostesses.

"Sir Breakfast?" I realized I was perversely staring at her. I had not seen a more beautiful woman in a long time. I was spellbound.

"Non-vegetarian! By the way what's for breakfast?"

"I think you will prefer the vegetarian breakfast; non-vegetarian is not your type." I was about to lose my temper but managed to keep my mouth shut.

She read my mind and answered "I know your choice in breakfast." Saying this she moved down the aisle.

She had handed me a vegetarian breakfast that I always preferred. I finished the tasteless cold food and went back to sleep. The announcement that we were about to land in Delhi woke me up. At the exit door Amita bid me goodbye with a smile, "Have a great day Sir in New Delhi."

****

Chapter 23

At the airport, Mr. Ramakrishna was waiting for me. I had never met him before but he recognized me.

"Welcome to Delhi, Mr. Prabuddh!" He extended his hand to greet me. I clutched his hand; I sensed warmness in his handshake.

"Pleased to meet you, Mr. Ramakrishna."

Mr. Ramakrishna was Tapasya's father. He was running a company that produced automobile parts. Tapasya was not happy when he divorced her mother. Tapasya was very close to his heart. He was very upset when he heard the news of her sad demise. He had tried to contact me many times but I remained oblivious to the outside world. This time I contacted him when I decided to come back into the business and to avenge Tapasya's death. He was excited to join me in my mission. He told me that he had made efforts to find out people responsible for Tapasya's death. He had even hired a professional detective to investigate her death. The detective had retrieved various photographs, videos and other important evidence that could lead to the suspect. Although Mr. Ramakrishna was quite powerful to unearth any conspiracy behind Tapasya's death but it seemed there was someone more influential and powerful who might have hindered his efforts during the last year. He felt our coming together will help solve the mystery.

"So what is the plan?" he asked me while driving to his home in Delhi.

"I was in despair and incommunicado for almost a year. First, I am going to regain my health. After that I want to start focusing my mind to devise a strategy."

"How?"

"I want a place where I can work and catch up on current trends of business and medical research market."

"I don't want you to monkey around; I want you to reveal who hurt my daughter."

"Mr. Ramakrishna, be patient. I want to do the same."

"When I heard first about it, I thought you might have killed her, but when I saw you at your bungalow crying for her…"

"Did you come to my home?"

"Yes, I would have killed you if I had not realized your love for her."

"I am also responsible for her death; I could not explain and clear some doubts she harbored about me."

"It was a total misunderstanding; you had tried your best but her childish nature led her to this problem. She should have trusted you instead of believing others." His voice cracked up remembering his daughter. "Someone created false evidence of your affairs. He must be someone very powerful person. Therefore, I extended my hand for help to combine our forces to fight this person."

"It could be Kaumudi."

"Do you have any other suspects?"

"Yes, but I need evidence."

"May I know someone you suspect?"

"Wait for some time Sir; let me work on it first." He wasn't too happy with my answer.

We reached his home. A large gate led to a palatial bungalow. The lawns looked beautiful with flowers and trees. He drove the car into the porch where we got off.

"Welcome to my little palace! This place was Tapasya's favorite. She used to play with Kaumudi here in the garden during her childhood."

"With Kaumudi?" My eyes popped out.

"Yes, when they were kids. Mr. Mehta was my business partner years ago; we had a nice mutual understanding and we were good friends. Kaumudi and Tapasya were childhood friends and had studied together in primary school."

"Tapasya had never told me about this."

"She might have told you if you had asked about her chemistry with Kaumudi. And she did not want you to take advantage of their friendship."

"Advantage of their friendship?"

"Kaumudi had already contacted Tapasya before she agreed to join you. She had all your past records from Tapasya and that was the reason she was ready to do business with you; both of them had a deal not to reveal their past relations with you."

"I thought she would hide nothing from me."

"But she loved you most."

"And how did you get to know all this; from your detective?"

"No, she shared everything with me; your first dinner together when she tied your hair in ponytail." Ramakrishna's face was smiling when he spoke about Tapasya. We had already reached the drawing hall where he made me comfortable in the sofas.

"She was quite a mischievous girl and Kaumudi too. She told me about your tough personality when she was joined your company. At one point of time, she did not want to continue with your company and asked for my advice. But I had heard good things about you so I advised her to continue. She was not too happy and was probably stressed out because she lost some important files."

He was continuously talking about Tapasya. I

was also enjoying his talk-I don't know why.

"Then next day she called to tell me that she was in love; she was amazed by your nice behavior. And do you know what she told me?" He burst out with laughter suddenly. I smiled reluctantly without any reason.

"She told me that papa Prabuddh has beautiful hair and I want to marry him to own his hair and to play with it every day." He stopped laughing, his eyes became wet and again misery covered his face, "but she is now…"

I tried to calm him and gave him a glass of water. "Mr. Ramakrishna everything will be OK. But we cannot bring her back. Your tears will torment her soul."

"Why did you separate from Mr. Mehta? Was there any dispute between you two?"

"No we had a partnership agreement demarcating the business. I had my automobile production and he had steel production. We never got in touch after that. I could not grow my business as I could not concentrate because of problems in relationship with my wife."

"Did you meet Kaumudi after…?" I left my question incomplete, hoping he would understand.

"She came to my home as soon as she heard the news; she also tried to contact you but you did not respond."

"Do you suspect her?"

"There is some evidence against her but I am not sure if I want to believe it. She had no reason to get her out of the way-either money or some other reason. She was happy with our relationship."

A maid brought some sandwiches. I was hungry and bit into the sandwiches. He also joined me.

"Tapasya told me that you married a rich woman!"

"Yes I did, but that was six months after she left me. I am living alone now."

"Why did she leave you?"

"She could not stand my crazy longing for Tapasya. She said I have become a psycho."

"Today she owns half of your property as compensation for divorce."

"Your doubt is obvious but she was richer than me and she demanded nothing in the divorce."

"Anyway I should leave now." I drank the remaining coffee.

"You have planned to stay with me at my home." He looked miserable again.

"Yes I had but I have just changed my plan. I have to find some quiet place that will let me work."

"I have many rooms and …"

"I am thankful to you and would be pleased to stay with you. But …"

"But you cannot work when her memories are all around you, right?" He was happy that he understood what I was thinking.

He arranged for a car to drop me at my hotel.

****

Chapter 24

In the hotel I switched on my laptop and went through the recently created website for the medical research agency. The website looked great. Apparently the website developer had done good work in a short time.

That evening I had an appointment with Dr. Arpan Acharya, the director of the medium sized company Acharya Ltd with an annual turnover of Rs. 100 crores. He was running the research agency for the last five years but was now facing a large financial crisis and wanted to sell a part of his company. He wanted to sell 40% of his shares to me. I offered him 35 crore rupees. We were to sign the deal today evening.

Dr. Arpan Acharya arrived at the meeting time. Contrary to my belief, he was a 30-year-old businessman, who had started the company after earning his MD Pharma degree. He was dressed in a dark suit paired with black shoes. I was as usual dressed in casuals-pink T-shirt, beige coloured denims and black loafers. My ponytail was tied in a brown hairband. I had already started working out and did almost 100 crunches every day to flatten my belly.

He was accompanied by Valmiki, one of the directors. They were both confused to see me in my casual look. I greeted them by their names. I had done my due diligence of the company and found no risk to invest in his company.

We took seats around the conference table.

"Here is the agreement." Arpan put the agreement papers on the table after formal introduction.

"Media reports say you have sold everything." Arpan wanted my reaction on the news.

"Let them say what they want to say." I started reading the papers. "It will take me few minutes to go through these papers. In the meantime, will you like to have some tea or coffee?" As a businessman I was always careful to go through any agreement before signing.

"No thanks, but can we trust you?" His words irritated me. I was about to lose my temper. I tried to calm myself down but could not hide the irritated expression on my face as I answered him.

"This should be my question and not yours. I am the one who is investing money in your company and taking risk." I put the papers back on the table and stretched back comfortably on the chair. The message was clear–either he stops his nonsense or risk seeing the deal cancelled.

"Sorry Sir, he did not mean anything like that. We completely trust you and your business acumen. We believe in you; having you on board will only take the company higher." Valmiki smelled the situation and tried to calm me down. Valmiki held 5% of shares in the company. It seemed both Valmiki and Arpan had good mutual understanding.

I looked at Mr. Arpan who reluctantly nodded and handed me back the papers. "My apologies! I am upset due to financial pressure and this company is my baby."

"It is OK, Mr. Arpan. I understand you have to bite the bullet sometime. But don't worry now, I am here to help you." I signed the agreement with a smile. Mr. Arpan was facing a maelstrom of emotions. I liked his possessiveness for his organization; now it was our organization.

"Mr. Acharya, now that we have signed the agreement, here is the cheque of Rs. 35 crores." I handed him a signed cheque drawn on State Bank of India. This is a transparent transaction and we don't need to hide anything from the government.

"Yes, one more thing; I will like to chair the meeting day after tomorrow. Please ask all your key persons to attend the meeting at 9:00 am." My communication was very professional and I wasn't sure how he would take it. "Our employees should be ready now for some slogging. And you should now take it easy. "We are in this together."

"It will be arranged, Sir." Valmiki replied. Only Arpan had sold his part of shares.

Valmiki was not rich enough to buy out Arpan's

share but he was quite supportive of Arpan. He was trustworthy and he was my link to approach Arpan. I had contacted him when I got the news of Arpan's financial crisis and offered to buy a part of the company. I had scrutinized this company among the best thirteen Indian research agencies based on growth potential and management. Arpan's business acumen and attitude attracted me to his company. My business contacts informed me about his financial crisis just two days back when I had decided to come back in business. I approached Valmiki and everything was smooth from there on.

****

Chapter 25

I went to washroom to freshen myself as both Arpan and Valmiki left the hotel room.

I changed into blue denim shirt and jeans paired with brown casual shoes.

I searched Amita's number on my phone's contact list and dialed her number.

"Hello!" Amita's sweet voice answered after four rings.

"Hi, I am Prabuddh and am I speaking with Amita?"

"Oh...Sir...I am so happy to hear from you. I can't believe you actually called me. I am so happy!" I was surprised to hear her reaction and the fact she still admired me. Although I was not exactly fat and ugly but I was not dashing looking either like before.

"Amita, will you do me a favor?" I cut in.

"Anything for you, Sir!"

"I need some place to live. Can you please arrange something?" I could have approached a broker but I did not know why I called Amita for help.

"Sorry Sir, but it will be really difficult to manage a bungalow appropriate for your status in Delhi on such a short notice."

"No, I don't need any large house; a small

apartment will do." That must have stunned her. This was a part of my plan. I was planning something very big and for that I was seeking a small place to reside in.

"Sir, I know a small place. But…" she hesitated.

"I want to go check it out. Do you have a contact number?" I did not let her complete the sentence.

"If you don't mind I am free now and can accompany you to the place."

"Are you sure?"

"Sure. Actually I will be glad to accompany you."

"Ok, then what time?"

"Sir where are you exactly now?"

"I am at Lodhi Hotel in Pragati Vihar."

"The hotel is a little far away from my place; I will pick you up in 45 minutes."

"Sure. So nice of you! Thank you again."

"You are always welcome Sir. See you in the visitor's lounge." She hung up.

I had seen Amita many times before but was never this attracted to her like now. I was losing control of my senses; this might create dangerous situations and spoil my whole plan. I must start meditation soon. I had planned to reside at Mr. Ramakrishna's home but his history of partnership with Mr. Mehta rained on my parade. I was planning to take over Mr. Mehta's company but his previous friendship might ruin my whole my plan.

I had been expanding my business very fast. Mr.

Mehta, once in a meeting, had given me a clue about marrying Kaumudi. I expressed my inability because I was in love with Tapasya. He knew if I would somehow lose Tapasya, Kaumudi will have a chance. He might have planned the whole thing that created doubt in Tapasya's mind that I was not to be trusted. Now was the time to take revenge for my love. I washed my face, combed my hair and tied them in ponytail to go with Amita.

****

Chapter 26

Amita was wearing a pink saree over her beautiful Indian curves. Her wide smile proved that she had noticed the glint in my eyes. Her smile was mesmerizing and the tone of her voice hypnotized me. I stood speechless seeing her in a saree. We sat in her new Maruti Baleno car.

"Should we go?" She interrupted my mesmerized silence and brought me to the present.

"What is our destination?"

"Dwarka Residency, about ten kilometers from here." She briefed me. I still could not talk. She had me under her spell.

"A 2BHK apartment is available in the building where I live with my colleague. If you happen to like the flat, we can be neighbours." She was choosing her words very carefully and had stressed on the word 'neighbours'.

"Who is the owner of the apartment?"

"I have spoken to him; he will meet us there."

"What will be the rent?"

"We are paying twenty thousand rupees for two persons. You can negotiate."

She suddenly braked as we hit a speed breaker that she noticed at the last moment.

"Sorry!"

"It is OK; your driving is not too bad for a female."

"So is it right what people talk about you?"

"What?"

"You have so many biased opinions about females."

"Most women drive cars recklessly."

"You believe so?" She frowned at me.

"You are driving faster than most F1 drivers!" I smiled, trying to repair the damage I might have caused. "Especially when it is difficult to drive wearing a saree."

"It is a very comfortable outfit."

"Might be. Oh I remembered, I have to buy some clothes for me."

"Mr. Billionaire has run out of clothes." She spoke sarcastically.

"Now I am not a billionaire."

"Sorry, I just watched the news on television; you had to sell everything."

"I don't want to discuss it now. Suggest me a good place where I can buy few clothes at reasonable cost."

"If you don't mind, I may accompany you to Connaught Place."

"I am blessed to have company of a beautiful girl like you."

"Sir, I am already impressed by you and I respect you. You don't need to flirt with me!" She was having fun with me. I really liked her honesty and confidence.

Her left hand moving the gear of the car touched my hand. A soft puffy feeling ran through my body. Feelings I have not felt in a long time tugged at me somewhere deep inside. I felt like a man again–a big dose of testosterone was flowing through my veins. I did not bother to move my hand. I had an intense craving to kiss her. I was sure she would notice it.

"Although, you are unlike any other men I know."

"Any normal man will lose heart to your beautiful smile and silky voice."

"Flirting is not allowed." She repeated.

"That is an honest appreciation from a pure heart."

"I have heard…"

"That I don't talk to girls. Is it?" I completed her sentence.

"But it seems that you are very experienced. OK,

here we are." We entered a small township like residential area. She found a place to park the car.

The locality was built in a ten-acre area. Ten high-rise blocks were built around a small garden. The garden contained a children's playground with slides and see-saws. On one side of the garden few wooden benches were installed.

"Only one unit is empty." She informed me.

"This way."

I followed her to the fifth floor of B Block. She preferred to climb the stairs instead of taking the elevator. I was panting when we got to the fifth floor. Rohan greeted Amita, "Hi Amita! I have been waiting for fifteen minutes."

"Rohan, sorry for the delay; you know Delhi traffic. Anyway, meet Mr. Prabuddh!"

"Hi Rohan, pleased to meet you."

"Mr. Prabuddh, Amita told me about you. Come in, this is the apartment. This is the main hall... this is master bedroom... this is another bedroom...this is the kitchen...this is washroom. Each bedroom contains attached toilet bathroom." Rohan was in hurry to show me the apartment.

The apartment was quite appropriate for my need. The garden below was visible from the window of the master bedroom.

"The construction is just a year old. The entire

apartment is fully furnished; you can shift here with a bag containing your clothes only."

"And how much it will cost me?"

"The rent is thirty thousand rupees per month." I looked at Amita.

"He will pay 25000 plus maintenance" She bargained for me.

"Amita, I don't want to bargain!"

"So 25000 per month, done." Amita declared with a smile.

No man on earth could deny a beautiful girl like Amita with her million-dollar smile.

"50000 advance; when will you shift here?"

"Tomorrow afternoon."

"Tomorrow morning we will complete the papers and handover you the key. Keep ready your identity proof and other documents with the advance money." He handed me his visiting card and locked the door. The entire meeting did not take more than 15 minutes.

"I will meet you tomorrow morning at 10:00 am." He departed and I was left alone with Amita.

Only a wall separated our houses; Amita's apartment was 503 and mine was 502.

"This is where I live-apartment 503, B Block,

Dwarka Township, Dwarka." She was standing before me after Rohan had left, pampering her mid back long loose hair with her slender fingers.

"I should leave now." I did not know how to react. I cursed myself for saying this instead of thanking her.

"If you don't mind, you can have a look inside while I prepare some tea." Saying this she unlocked her apartment and walked inside without waiting for my reply. She knew I would definitely follow her inside, which I did.

****

Chapter 27

Amita had a well maintained apartment. The hall had sofas with matching curtains. The walls were green and the wall which had the LED television was painted in the colours of a forest.

"You have a nice place. You girls really live neatly; hard for us bachelors to live like this."

"You can rest here. Will you like tea or coffee?" She pointed the sofa to me but I caught her eyes staring at my feet and annoyance on her face. She had removed her heels at the door while I had walked in with my shoes spoiling her red carpet. Well I did tell her we boys don't know how to keep our houses clean!

"Oh sorry, I should remove my shoes." I removed my shoes outside and again marched to the sofas.

While walking to the sofa I noticed a painting through the open door of one of the bedrooms; was it the same painting or an illusion? It would be odd to look into her bedroom just to check the painting. She was preparing tea in the kitchen, but the glimpse of the painting had triggered a storm of thoughts in my mind.

'It was a painting by my grandmother Sumitradevi, who was a well-known painter. During her last days when she was 70 years old, she had completed her last painting. I was her model, a seven-year-old child. We were in forest of Gir where she had made me sit on a rock lying in midst of trees. I don't exactly remember everything but she had taken seven hours to complete the painting. The painting *was a master piece of her life; she would not have sold it for anything. The next day she left for her heavenly abode. She had handed over the painting to my father and wanted my father to keep it forever. During the tough times when Papa needed money to save mummy, he had to sell the painting with a heavy heart.'*

"Here is the tea. I think you will like the lemon tea with these roasted peanuts." She brought me back to the world.

"Thanks, you have a good collection of paintings." She handed me the tea and sat down.

She was a little confused. She looked at me for some clarification.

"I had a glimpse of the painting in your bedroom."

"You are talking about '*City Boy in the Forest*'; it was gifted by my parents on my 16th birthday. They had purchased it in an auction. The painting is a masterpiece of Sumitradevi. I don't know much about paintings but this painting is my parents' remembrance."

"I am so sorry!" *Yes, this was my grandmother's painting.* I had thought of buying the painting but now it was quite difficult.

"It is OK. I am proud of my parents. My father died with his boots on. He was in the army. My mother was fond of painting and she died of heart attack. She dreamt of seeing me married during her lifetime but she could not…" I finished the tea with some peanuts. She poured out her heart to me. I don't have the social skills to offer condolences;

especially girls. There was some silence while she wiped her tears quietly.

I pretended that I did not see her cry. "Your parents would be proud of their bold and brave girl; where ever they are" she smiled reluctantly.

"My roommate tells me that I am innocent looking, and many men have complimented my beauty; but you are the first one to compliment me for being a brave girl."

"You are innocent, beautiful and brave living your life in this difficult world all alone, even as you face piercing gazes." I paused. She was hanging on to every word I was saying. "Even I had been staring at you like a desperate man all this while. I apologize for my behavior."

She was speechless. I could not raise my eyes; ashamed of myself. I stood up ready to leave her apartment without speaking any word.

"Don't you want to see the painting of your own grandmother?" The words shocked me and I almost lost my balance tying my shoelaces. I stood up, still shocked. She smiled kindly like an angel.

"I know this is your painting. My mother was the student of your granny. She did not want this painting to go into hands of a stranger, so she bought it when your father put it in an auction. She told me one day the boy in the painting would come to you, and here you are."

I was standing before her still speechless. This was a day of surprises.

"Come on hurry up, before I change my mind little boy."

I swiftly removed my shoes, and excitedly followed her inside.

Yes, it was the same painting and it was me sitting on the rock, smiling innocently. Grandmother had rendered my face perfectly. Emotions of excitement on my face were perfectly juxtaposed with expressions of my restlessness of childhood. I could gaze into my large black eyes. My hair had the same shiny texture. My little hands were drawing in the ground while my forehead was smeared with dirt. She even painted the ant that had bitten me and I had screamed of fear.

In the background of the green dense forest, I was a little city boy wearing a pink frock, that she had gifted, with my hair tied with a pink bow. When I refused to wear those girly things, she kissed me on my cheeks and said, "These are just clothes; they do not have any gender. Gender is in the mind of people, and the thought of gender in mind corrupts the divine energy the God Almighty has given to humans. Never fall in the trap of 'this is for boy and this for girl'. From today whenever you see this painting, you will recall these words that will clear your heart, your thoughts and your acts. This painting will give you energy to fight against all evil."

I had not understood her words then and reluctantly wore the clothes to obey her; but today I understood her words and the message of the painting.

Drops of tears fell on my bare feet; the wetness of the tears running on my face pulled me back to the present. I realized that I was standing in the bedroom of a girl, staring at the painting for a long time; speechless and lost in thought.

"I am really thankful for your kindness Amita."

She stared at me for a minute. I did not want to make things uncomfortable.

"I should leave now; I need to do some shopping." I paused for a while and left the bedroom; she followed me.

"It will be really nice if you can spare me some more time. And maybe you can drop me at my hotel." I was being selfish.

"Wait for ten minutes, let me get ready."

After ten minutes she appeared before me wearing the same saree; I could not figure out what she spent ten minutes on. We were on our way to shop.

****

Chapter 28

She had great fashion sense and bargaining power. After two hours of tiring shopping, I bought few pairs of formal attire. She could not resist herself and also bought a top; the latest offering of 'Ponytail'. I noticed 'Ponytail' dominated the fashion industry and now had expanded to personal grooming. For a moment I thought of Kaumudi.

We were seated in a restaurant for dinner after our shopping expedition. She had ordered some sizzlers along with cheese corn soup.

"I don't know what I would have done if you had not come with me."

"You men never stop flirting."

"Really, I am being honest. You have very good fashion sense."

"Ok, thanks for the appreciation." She flashed a fabricated smile.

I remained silent while I finished the soup. The waiter set down the plates for main course.

"So is Mr. Billionaire hurt?" She teased me again.

"My name is Prabuddh."

"Mr. Prabuddh Sir!"

"I thought we are friends now, and if you also think so, you can address me as Prabuddh." I picked a piece of mushroom from the sizzler with my fork without raising my eyes.

"Prabuddh is a nice name; may I ask who thought of such a different name for you?" she was trying to pull me back into conversation.

"My grandmother." I answered gruffly and continued to stuff my mouth with the food. She had finished her soup and food was being served to her. She was trying to elevate my mood; I was enjoying her efforts.

"You have very nice and silky long hair; although the way you have tied them in half ponytail is feminine but it looks very pretty on you. Who taught you to make ponytail?" She reminded me of Tapasya; my hand froze midway in the air. For a moment Tapasya's face flashed in my mind; her smiling, charming face, her light hearted talks, the moments of intimacy we had and then finally her swollen face.

"Prabuddh, I am sorry if my words have hurt you." Amita offered me handkerchief to wipe my tears that had unknowingly overflowed from my eyes.

"Tapasya taught me to tie my ponytail." I tried to answer her question; I was feeling embarrassed. It was for the first time that I was getting emotional in front of a girl whom I hardly knew. I had already cried twice in this brief meeting.

"I have heard name of the girl you were in

relationship with; I am sorry."

"Actually I am a very tough person but I don't know how you managed to make me emotional twice in a span of three hours."

"It is your love for granny and Tapasya." There was a heavy silence again.

"Actually, you look very cute when you become emotional." She giggled, "I like boys like you who can express emotions honestly."

"I am already impressed by you Miss Air Queen; no need to flirt with me." It was my tit-for-tat comment to lighten the mood.

Amita lived alone in New Delhi, dreaming of a successful marriage life, had affairs twice in her college life which ended for whatever reasons. Now she was looking for a mature man who will take care of her, give her respect and who would also be able to afford her expenses. I did not have skills to get her to talk about herself; she herself opened up to me.

After I paid for the dinner, she dropped me at my hotel. Next day she had a busy flight schedule, so she promised to meet me the day after I shifted to her neighbor apartment.

****

Chapter 29

Rohan was a professional and a nice guy. Dealing with him was easy and the formality was completed with ease. He handed me the apartment after we signed an eleven months contract. Because the apartment was fully furnished moving in was easy with just a bag of clothes and my laptop. Rohan introduced me to Ketakiben, who had been taking care of various cleaning and other chores. I hired her for all home chores except cooking.

Amita's flat was closed when I shifted to my new residence. My phone rang just before lunch time.

Her name flashed as I picked up the phone. "Hello!" I answered.

"May I talk to Mr. Prabuddh?" A familiar lady voice asked formally.

"Yes, Miss Kaumudi; this is Prabuddh."

"Thank God, you recognized me Prabuddh. Where are you? I am not talking to you; you did not even call me after coming to Delhi." She almost chided me.

"I wanted to give you a surprise."

"Liar, whatever; where are you now? Let us meet for lunch."

"Somewhere in Dwarka."

"Send me your complete address, and be ready. I will come and pick you up in half hour."

"OK sure, bye, see you." I disconnected the call and sent her the full address. After an hour we were having lunch in one of the royal hotels of Delhi amidst cool and quiet environs.

"So what are you going to set up?" Kaumudi started the conversation. I was meeting her after a long time; she still had the same magnetic personality.

"I have not decided yet; I have lost my confidence and do not have guts to start my own business again. I am looking for a job." I answered looking down at my food.

She put her hand below my chin raising it and looked into my eyes and asked "When are you joining 'Ponytail'?"

Her action was unexpected; I did not say anything. I just conveyed a confused expression, and then freed my chin from her hand.

"I sold you everything."

"I know but you have the right to join the company. I can get the Managing Director post for you." She said sympathetically.

I smiled weakly; the cheer did not reach my eyes.

"I know it is not up to your level. But unfortunately, I alone cannot offer you the partnership; but…"

"Thank you for your kindness; I am glad you thought of me."

"You did not answer my question."

"I am not used to working under anyone, but I have no other option."

"So now the ponytail will fly again in the sky with the news of your comeback."

"Hope so. Thanks for your support in my tough time."

"You have put on much weight." She changed the topic suddenly.

"I have started working out again and the efforts will show in a month, Madam."

"Madam?"

"It's a habit."

"Stop taunting me. I know you suspect me for the loss of Tapasya and …" I did not understand why she suddenly broached the topic. She was apparently disturbed with something.

"I am not…"

"See you don't sound convincing; you actually doubt me. Otherwise you would have called me before coming to Delhi and have met me first." She was almost angry and now she was getting emotional.

"I swear I don't Kaumudi; but I was not sure whether you will meet me or not."

"We were friends Prabuddh; not just business partners. And how dare you think like that? I don't want to talk to you now anymore." She made a face.

"Why I could not see this inner beauty before?"

'Chand jaise ruth kar hamase badalo ke piche chup gaya, Galati ham se bas itini hui ki na samaj paye chand ko.'

(Moon is upset and has hidden behind the clouds; my only mistake was that I could not understand it)

The poet inside me was there to amuse her.

"Wow, you write poetry too! Please I want to hear more." That always worked; girls always love poetry.

"Where is the arrogant girl I knew before?"

"The girl disappeared in the air as the poet appeared before me."

"We are talking like love birds." I could not control my laugh.

"Prabuddh, I dream of you as my…" she kept staring in my eyes. Her facial expression had changed; her glossy lips were wet and her eyes became more mysterious. She was shivering with emotions. Seeing her like this I stopped laughing. Even time seemed to have stopped. Her eyes were talking in silence.

I took her hand in my hand. She looked thrilled; I could feel her emotions now.

"Kaumudi!"

"I know you love Tapasya, but I love you too." Her shivering disappeared as if her energy came out of her body in the form of words.

I clenched her hand more tightly, my magnetic smile flashed again on my face; "I love you too."

"You have lightened my heart."

"Actually I liked Tapasya, but I loved you from our first day. My arrogance did not allow me to confess."

I knew what I was doing. She was lost in my eyes. She might have heard but not understood my words.

"Kaumudi, I want to say something." I tried to bring her back to world.

"Say it again." She was smiling shyly; her cheeks had turned red. Her voice had a different sweetness to it. I had never seen that expression before.

"Kaumudi, I love you too."

"Again." She laughed.

"I love you too."

"Again!"

I moved my chair closer, slipped my hands around her neck and picked hair strands from her face. Her heart was throbbing and beating hard; anybody could have heard her heartbeats from a distance. She was staring at me, speechless, lost in my eyes.

Our lips came closer and we could feel each other's breath on our faces. My mouth drooled with the promise of her pouty and shiny red lips. I was just about to kiss her when I withdrew myself.

"Why did you stop?" She felt like I dropped her midway.

"Onions…I had onions, and…"

She burst into laughter. I also joined her; other customers looked at us acting silly.

****

Chapter 30

"Everything is as plan, Ahmad. Keep me updated about Prajwalit Ltd. And I have just shared few important documents with you; study them and give your views by tonight."

I hung up and shut off the laptop in my new bedroom. It was 8:00 pm. Kaumudi had signed me as the Managing Director of 'Ponytail' and then arranged to have me dropped in Dwarka. I was not in a mood to cook so decided to go out for dinner.

I removed my T-shirt. The exercises were bringing in the desired changes. My abdomen looked flat. I posed to see my biceps and pectorals. I was enjoying seeing my body getting into shape again.

The phone rang to interrupt my enjoyment; it was Dr. Arpan Acharya. I was thinking of calling him after dinner but he had called to confirm the meeting at his office.

He wanted to arrange a press conference, and officially announce to media about my investment in his business.

"Dr. Arpan, I understand your view and excitement; but it would be better for our business not to make any official public announcement. And if possible, keep it a secret from your employees too. Although I have started to work for your company but it would be better if the meeting involves only key persons."

"But Mr. Prabuddh…"

"Trust me. I am concerned about our business. Have trust in me and do as I tell you."

"OK Prabuddh, but be careful this company is my dream and my life." His voice was tired and lacked confidence.

"Arpan, you will soon realize that you are partnering the best entrepreneur. But I need your trust in me to keep our partnership a secret." The doorbell rang before I could complete the sentence.

"OK see you tomorrow."

"See you." I hung up and opened the door.

A lady was standing before me, tired and infuriated; she extended her hand to give me a box, "Amita asked me to give you this."

"Thank you, but you are…" I took the box.

"Patanjali, Amita's roommate. She is on duty today; so she called me to give you this lunchbox."

"Please come in." I turned into a gentleman. She looked at me from toe to head and smiled ruefully; I gathered I was standing bare chest with loose long hair.

"Sorry, just a minute!" I swiftly put on a T-shirt and again welcomed her.

"It is OK. The box contains fried rice, with mi veg subji that I have prepared" She went back to h flat.

****

Chapter 31

After the dinner I went for a walk in the garden of the society.

The garden was full of people on this cheerful and cool evening. Few people were strolling around the garden while children played. Few couples occupied the wooden benches. A group of four middle aged men were busy in some discussion in the center of the garden.

I inhaled the fresh and clear air and walked leisurely on the jogging path. I was enjoying the cheer of people around celebrating their family lives.

I came to the place where the children were playing in the garden. I sat on the green grass with my arms holding my legs bent at the knee watching them play.

Their play reminded me of my childhood...

"Prabuddh jump, don't fear; I will catch you!" Papa cajoled me standing below.

"I will fall down papa, I am your only child and I am just ten years old. I don't want to jump." I was scared of jumping from the pole on which I was hanging where papa had hung me on to do pull ups. I could count up to two only and by that time he had left me hanging on the pole. And now he wanted me to jump from the pole; perhaps the ground was two or three feet below my feet.

"Jump!" he shouted. I was trembling with fear but there was no way out. I closed my eyes for a moment and then raising my head, looked at the sky. The sky had turned into fire by the setting sun. I again looked down at the ground and then at papa. I felt numb. My mind felt like vacuum with all my thoughts sucked out leaving a large empty hole. I sensed rather than heard papa screaming below.

I looked at the pole, gathered all my strength in the shoulders, swung myself in the air, and then released the pole. For a moment I was suspended in the air.

The time had stopped for me as I felt the air rushing through my hair. I opened my eyes and saw myself flying in the sky; fear of falling down was gone. I spread my arms, brought my feet together bending them at the knees, spun myself into a somersault in the air and landed safely on my flat feet.

Papa ran to me, "Brave boy, I am so proud of you! You will make my name in future." He was smiling.

We went home after my adventure in the garden. He served aloo parathas in two plates with curd. As mummy was out for some social function, he had prepared parathas for both of us.

The phone rang. He picked up the phone listening intently to the person on the other end. His face turned hard. "Sir, I have collected enough evidence against the devil; if you allow I can throw Mr. Mehta behind prison bars."

****

Chapter 32

"Hi, are you the new man in society?" a male voice brought me back from the past. I turned my head; four men were standing around me. I could see curiosity in their eyes along with some hesitation.

"We saw you sitting here and came to talk to you. We are sorry if we have disturbed you." One of the men in the group wearing a loose kurta apologized.

"No problem! Nice to meet you all! By the way I am Prabuddh." I stood up and greeted them all with a smile.

They reciprocated and shook hands with me introducing themselves.

It has been a long time since I was meeting someone casually without any business interest. Almost all of them knew nothing about me except that I was there to find a job and Amita had recommended my name for the apartment.

Mahavir took the lead in talking once the introductions were over. "Amita is very sharp and well behaved girl and she has a good reputation in the society. If she has recommended your name, it means you must be her near relative or a very close friend."

Mahavir who seemed about 45-50 years old was the eldest of all. Himanshu and Rajendra were older than me. Kandarbh, the fourth man, was looking

younger than me.

"We are not relatives but are good friends. Her mother learnt painting from my grandmother." I spoke the plain truth. I did not know the guys very well.

"You must be in some creative field!" Mahavir was the inquisitive one. He knew how to talk to strangers. Maybe my long hair prompted him to ask that question.

"I work in the fashion and textile industry." I answered carefully.

"Ponytail? Did you work in Ponytail?" Kandarbh jumped in.

I was happy that someone could identify me even after one year.

"Did you say your name was Prabuddh? Oh God! You are the one; I don't believe my eyes. Please tell me this is not a dream; I am meeting the great Prabuddh!" Kandarbh was excited like a child.

"Kandarbhji, this is not a dream. Yes, I am Prabuddh, who owned Ponytail and Prajwalit Ltd. And now I am here to join Ponytail again."

"Mahavirji, he is the businessman who shook the business world few years back. But after that he disappeared for a year." Kandarbh could not control his excitement.

"Oh, so you must be a rich man. I don't

understand why you would want to live in this middle class society?" Mahavir interrogated me.

"You might have read in the newspapers about the sad turn of events. I am trying to stabilize again."

"Yes, I read that you lost your girlfriend and then passed your time like an insane ..." This time it was Rajendra's turn to blurt out but when he realized that he should not have used the word 'insane,' he left the sentence incomplete. There was an uncomfortable silence after his blunder. To put everyone back to ease I smiled, making an attempt to show them that the word did not hurt me. "Obviously my long hair and such bizarre stories will create an image that you will all believe whatever the newspapers say."

I summed up for them my life story adding that I was joining 'Ponytail' again tomorrow.

They all heard my story with wonder. Now they were full of sympathy for the man who lost his girlfriend and sold all his assets.

"What did you do with the money you got by selling your part in the company?" Mahavir was still not satisfied.

"A businessman carries a large debt. A huge part of the money went in paying off the debt. Rest is in my bank account.

"Do you have enough savings for your life time expenditure?"

"Yes, I do. Even if I stop working the money in the bank is enough for me to live a comfortable life. Anyway, I have shared everything about my life. Mahavirji, please tell me something about yourself."

"Mahavirji is the secretary of our society and he teaches English literature in college. He is the most respected member of this society." Himanshu praised Mahavir.

Hearing his praise Mahavir's eyes sparkled. Now I could divert the topic of conversation away from me.

"That is great, so you live and work among the young brigade of our country."

"I teach and mentor the young blood. Although people only criticize them but today's young generation is quite brilliant."

"Young generation is hard working, open minded and receptive." Kandarbh added. Half an hour passed as we discussed cricket, politics and current trends.

I was duly advised about many things-what to do and what not to do. I was cautioned against the bad members of the society and was made familiar with the different characters of various people of the society.

Then we walked out into the street to enjoy some tea at a road side stall. Our discussions continued. Last time I had tea at a road side stall was when I was in management school.

In my new life, new members entered who were neither business colleagues nor my relatives. They were my neighbors who could become good friends in the near future.

****

Chapter 33

I addressed a meeting of key persons of Acharya Ltd with Arpan and Valmiki. It was a short introduction of the managing staff of our pharma research agency. Arpan and Valmiki provided me more inputs as we took a round of their research unit.

The research unit had few small cabins where subjects for various clinical experiments were accommodated. Each cabin accommodating a single human subject was equipped with life supporting system and other necessary medical equipment. After the round they took me to the office of chief medical officer who was a dynamic young person. He was quite busy and could hardly spare few minutes for us.

That was my first and only strange experience of how a man could not spare time for his employer.

"Dr. Parmar is an intelligent asset of our company. Though he looks very young, he is 40 years old and is a bachelor. He has devoted his whole life to the medical research field. He has such a reputation that any agency in the world would pay him whatever he wants." Arpan told me after we were out of the office.

"So why has he been continuing with our company?"

"Our policy, Prabuddh; we do not put any restrictions on his work. We let him work on his own accord. And you would know that intelligent people have weird behavior and unusual manners."

"And that is why he did not prefer to meet us today morning?"

"He had an appointment for video conference with some scientist in New York."

"Quite impressive! We can definitely use his skills and knowledge in future also."

After discussing the policies of the company, Dr. Arpan escorted me to my car. We had decided to meet after two days. Till that time, I was to study various aspects of the business with the materials and documents he had provided me.

****

Chapter 34

I joined 'Ponytail' again as the Managing Director. Mr. Mehta was happy with my comeback.

I was allotted a chamber in the main office. Kaumudi called me to her office in the afternoon.

"May I come in?" I knocked the door and asked for her permission. She was on call so nodded her head and signalled me to take a seat. She was talking to a friend, "I will call you later on; I have some emergency meeting."

"So how was your first day?"

"Busy but exciting; you have made many appreciative changes in the company."

"I am bored of work, let's go somewhere for coffee."

"I thought you had some important work for me."

"It is important for you to keep me happy." She narrowed her eyes mischievously and bit her lip.

"I have lots of file to go through on my table but..."

"But?" I stood up from the chair, walked around the table towards her, and sat on the table. She held her breath in anticipation. I put my hand around her neck and pulled her slowly so that our faces were close to each other. Her hands held my face. Her quivering lips met mine. She sucked my lips furiously making moaning sounds. Her sudden passion was quite unexpected. I was fighting for breath. After having her fill she let me go. I could finally breathe. She stared in my eyes for some time and then rose from her chair. Now my head was at the level of her shoulder. She removed the hairband from my hair and grasped them, pulling me down and raising my chin. She smiled slightly, and asked me, "What did you decide-to work or to date me?"

"Because my boss wants me to date her, I have to do what she wants."

She released my hair, pulled my cheek and said, "Baby, you are so cute!"

"I never thought you were so naughty."

"Ok, let us go." She started to wind up her files.

"I will meet you in ten minutes in the parking lot." I stood up.

"Prabuddh!"

"Tie your hair before you go out of my office."

I almost forgot about our little adventure. I made up my hair and straightened my clothes and walked out of the door.

She drove me to a lake, on the bank of which, few benches were set. It was a sunny evening of winters. The place looked like a picnic spot. Because it was not a holiday, instead of family crowd, only few young couples were there.

The water of the lake was clear and the place was well maintained. Food stalls lined up on one side. A group of boys and girls was enjoying some fast food.

"Nice place." I was exhilarated.

"I know, my friend recommended this place." After a pause of few seconds she continued, "Have you ever been here before?" We were sitting on the sandy ground; the water was just few steps away.

I turned my face towards her; she was looking at the water.

'She wants to know whether I was here before with Tapasya.'

Her question clouded my mind. I gathered the memory when Tapasya wished to come here and we spent some time here. But that was past.

I was looking at Kaumudi and she was looking at the water. I did not speak till my silence compelled her to turn her face and look at me.

"What? I did not get you."

She smiled without any charm. She did not like my answer; now she needed to speak her mind.

"Anyways if you don't want to tell me; let it go."

I took her hand in my hands, "Kaumudi, it is true that I loved Tapasya. I also love her today and will love her for my whole life. I passed my whole year in her memory; to live without her is difficult for me. But your love has strengthened me to live without her."

She smiled with glee in her eyes and joy returned to her body. She clenched my hand and kissed it.

She asked me to put my head in her lap. I did so. She untied my hair caressing them and my forehead.

"So you love two girls, but people say a person loves only once in a life." She asked me while playing with my hair. I remembered my mother. I closed my eyes.

"But you proved them wrong; and compelled me to fall in love again."

"I never knew this romantic side." She stopped caressing my head.

"My mother; your lap brings back my mother's memory."

"She always caressed my hairs and head lovingly whenever I was tired or crying."

"You and crying?" she was amused.

I opened eyes, "Of course, at the time I was ten years old."

"Do you think you have grown up?"

"Don't you think so?"

"No you are still a child, a workaholic child-a child who has grown his hair and has a muscular body but still keeps playing. The difference is that before you were playing with toys and now with money and feelings."

"Keep doing it."

"My hand is tired; get up from my lap."

"Now you are behaving like a child." I closed my eyes again and kept my head forcefully in her lap, even as she was trying to move my head.

"We are not so young to behave like other young couples."

"We are not so old either not to behave like them."

"Are you getting up or not?"

"No! I am not; if you want you can move my head from your lap."

"Are you sure? And if I succeed, what will be my reward then?"

"A surprise; I will give you a surprise gift."

"What will you give me?"

"It is surprise, sweetheart. But what if you do not succeed?"

"That is never going to happen; I will definitely succeed." She smiled mischievously as she gathered my hair in her hand and pulled them.

"It hurts!" I yelped in pain and raised my head from her lap.

"You are a cheater; I will never let you play with my hair again."

"I win. Where is my gift?" She was fully mischievous.

I pushed her down on the sand. The sand seemed like a chilled bed. The colour of the sky was turning red like a bedroom nightlight. It was cold but the temperature between us was rising. The waves rippled with rhythmic sound.

She submitted herself to me. We lay together. I brushed her hair from her face with my right hand. I reached forward to kiss her lips when she shyly turned her face towards the sky. Her right cheek was touching my lips. My lips glided over her soft face until they found her delicate right earlobe. I took her earlobe between my lips and nibbled at it. My tongue then found its way into her ear. She shook with pleasure as her nails dug into my hands.

"Oh my God! Where did you learn this?" She moaned in my ear.

As she turned her face again to me to talk, I grabbed her lips. After her ear, this time her lips got my attention. I sucked her firm lips and ran my tongue over her mouth. I gave her no chance to speak. The only sound was the furious slurps emanating from our mouths as we melted into each other's arms. We realized we were out in the open when the mosquitoes started to sing in our ears. We left the place when the mosquitoes started to bite. We were not too willing to be dinner for them.

****

Chapter 35

I was in the shower when the doorbell rang.

"Who is it? I am in bathroom!" I shouted.

"Hey Prabuddh, this is me!" I tried to recognize the voice-it was Amita.

I quickly came out of the bathroom, changed clothes and opened the door to see a smiling face behind the door.

"Hi Amita! Long time. Please come in." I greeted her and asked her to sit.

"Sorry, but could not meet you since you shifted here. By the way, how is everything going?" She asked sipping the water that I offered her.

"It is a nice place and I am settling down quickly. People are quite friendly. And I am thankful for your help to get this apartment."

"Mahavirji met me this evening; he was praising you. He said you met them last evening."

"Yes, I interacted with Mahavirji and other guys in the garden yesterday evening. They seemed like good people. Will you like to have something?"

She grinned. Her laugh embarrassed me. "You are so formal. I will have some cold coffee."

"Make yourself comfortable." I went into the kitchen, poured some cold milk into the shaker and added sugar and coffee.

While I was fussing around, Amita walked in. "I got bored outside. If you don't mind, may I help you?" Her act reminded me of Tapasya again. Despite my best efforts I could not forget Tapasya. Every time I tried to involve myself with others she would spring into my mind.

"I don't mind but everything is in control here." I tried to cheer up myself.

"Wow you have kept the kitchen neat and clean. I am impressed."

I grinned in response and handed her a cup of cold coffee. She was leaning on the kitchen platform.

"This tastes nice! You are an all-rounder-successful entrepreneur, nice human, good cook and…"

"And?"

"You might have some more skills that I don't know about yet." We finished our coffee and walked out into the main hall.

"So how is your work going?"

"I have joined 'Ponytail' again as the Managing Director."

"Congratulations!" she extended her hand.

"Thanks, and how is your work? You must have been busy these last two days."

"Yes, I had a busy schedule but tomorrow I have an off."

"You look tired."

"Hmmm, I just came back home two hours ago and took a bath. Patanjali is not here and I wanted to speak to someone. Luckily I found you at home. I hope I am not boring you."

"No, not at all! You are good company. How can anyone be bored in your company?" I reclined on the sofa. Her eyes were glued to my neck looking at the love bite I got in the evening.

"Mosquito bite." I did not know why I gave her an explanation. She smiled sarcastically. At the same time a message flickered on my mobile, 'Hi baby, what are you doing?'

'Hanging out with a friend, will call you later.' I texted.

"Seems like you had an interesting day in office!" Amita winked.

"Yes, it was quite an interesting day." I read her cues but maintained a straight face.

"Come on, you can tell me about it; I am your friend." She was jumping on the sofa like a kid. I did not expect her to be so much interested in gossip.

"What? It was just a routine day in the office."

She was not convinced by my answer. "I am not a

child; I can differentiate between love bite and mosquito bite. And I don't think you are a person to have pinky with any girl."

"Pinky-what is that?"

"Oh, that is a code word for hanky-panky. And now don't tell me that you have never heard of hanky-panky."

"You girls are really..."

"What really? Don't dare to say anything about girls; I am proud to be a girl." She said rising in defense of women.

"Really intelligent!" I wanted to end the discussion.

"That is cool. Now don't change the topic-who is that girl?"

"Of course, you are that girl!" She was shocked and her eyes popped out. I realized my blunder and tried to patch up the situation. "Between us, you are the girl-an intelligent girl." And I made an innocent face.

"Ha...ha... ha.... Very funny! I meant who is the lucky girl who gave you this love bite." She wanted me to shout from the rooftop about my relationship with Kaumudi.

"I told you it is not a love bite." I was not going to change my statement!

"Let me see!" She came up to me and uncovered my neck to have a better look of the mark.

'What the hell is she doing?' I had a closer look of her face; her tired face was pretty attractive. Her body smelled of soap. The innocence in her eyes mesmerized me. But my eyes were glued to her voluptuous bosom spilling out of her pink tank-top. My jaw fell.

She caught my eyes and withdrew herself. It was an awkward moment that left both of us embarrassed. I cursed myself for ogling at her.

We were saved by the bell–my phone rang bringing the awkward moment to a close.

"Excuse me!" I went outside in the balcony. It was Ahmad on the phone. Ahmad had gone through the papers that I had sent him, and briefed me about the financial status of Acharya Ltd. He had also mailed me the report.

When I returned to the hall, Amita was playing with her hair and surfing on the mobile.

"Sorry. It was my colleague."

"Do you work at night too?"

"Don't you?" I thanked God for the change of topic.

"My case is different."

"I know I am workaholic."

"And that is why you were successful then and now again you are going to rock the business world." Her phone flashed a message. "I should leave now. Patanjali is home; enjoyed talking with you."

"Same here!"

When she was at the door she turned back and said, "I think it was really a mosquito bite and…"

"And?"

"You will look more handsome in short hair, although this is not bad either. See you soon."

'Hi!' I texted Kaumudi after Amita had left.

'So finally you get the time to talk to me?'

'My neighbor was here to talk with me.'

'This long?'

'She was alone at her home, bored and wanted to talk with someone?'

'She?'

'Yes, Amita is her name. She is an airhostess and she helped me to find this apartment.'

'Hmmm… So you have texted me to talk about your new girlfriend.' The message was followed by emoji of angry expression.

'No it's not so. I have texted to let you know everything in my life.'

'And Amita is new chapter in your life, isn't it?'

'You are jealous!'

'I am not.'

'You are.'

'Why should I be jealous?'

'Because I spoke with a girl.'

'You are really a bad person.'

'Sweetheart, she is only a friend; a good friend. Nothing else.'

'I don't want to discuss her anymore.

'And what are you doing now?'

'I am... missing you...'

'And?'

'And chatting with a man.' We exchanged romantic sweet nothings for another half hour. It was already 10:00 pm. The love drama with Kaumudi was taking too much time. I had to compromise with my working hours. I wanted to work on Acharya Ltd. But I was feeling sleepy.

I switched off the lights and lay on the bed. I usually fell asleep in ten minutes but thoughts were swirling in my mind.

****

Chapter 36

As time went by, Kaumudi and I spent more and more time with each other; not only during office hours but also after office hours.

On the other hand, Amita was more than a good friend. I shared with her many things; things that I did not share with Tapasya or Kaumudi. I confessed to Amita about my relationship with Kaumudi. That did not affect our friendship; instead I and Amita grew close with time.

One day Kaumudi demanded to meet Amita. Surprisingly Amita agreed too. I was anxious that Sunday evening when we were all supposed to meet. The plan was to see a romantic Bollywood movie and then to have dinner.

I drove with Amita to the decided location.

She turned on the radio. The station was playing song from '*Sanam Re*' movie.

"Have you ever watched a movie in your life?" Amita asked me.

"Of course I have; during my college days."

"So you are going to watch a movie after a long time."

"Yes, thanks to you both ladies."

"Who do you love more?" I looked at Amita bewildered.

"I meant Kaumudi or Tapasya?" she was taking advantage of our friendship. I did not answer her and sped along the road. Her questions were hurting me. I could not forget Tapasya. She asked a question with which I had been grappling with lately.

"It is OK, if you don't want to talk about it."

"I still love Tapasya but that does not mean I am cheating on Kaumudi. She also has a place in my heart. Tapasya was past and Kaumudi is present. And the truth is that I will never forget Tapasya."

"If suppose by chance, Tapasya was to appear before you; who will you choose-Tapasya or Kaumudi?"

"Amita, Tapasya is no more in this world but she is still in my heart."

"You did not answer me."

"Tapasya, I will choose Tapasya."

"And where do I stand in your life?"

"At the same place where I stand for you-where close friends stand for each other.

"You are more than a friend to me but I know you love Kaumudi. My bad luck." She grinned. We were at the multiplex where Kaumudi was to meet us.

"Although I can change my mind, if you are ready to marry me." I tried to pull her leg.

"Good attempt but I will never marry a man who had hair longer than me." She gave it back to me. Kaumudi appeared at the entrance of the multiplex.

I introduced the ladies to each other. Soon the girls were talking like long lost friends. I recalled a similar situation few years back when Kaumudi had met with Tapasya. Both girls had forgotten me and that we were here to watch a movie.

"Sorry to interrupt you beautiful ladies but we are getting late for the movie." I waved the movie tickets in my hands.

"Oh sure!" Both grinned as we made our way to the theatre.

The movie was a typical Bollywood romantic story. The girls kept chattering throughout the movie.

Fortunately, I did not have any awkward situation but rather enjoyed the beautiful evening with the two lovely ladies.

****

Chapter 37

In the midst of being busy in relationships, my efforts and changes in the policy saved Acharya Ltd. The company was stable, and its valuation had increased. Dr. Arpan was happy with the growth the company showed in just few months. My involvement in 'Ponytail' was also effective and now it was one of the top brands that made Kaumudi one of the richest women in India.

One beautiful evening Kaumudi planned a dinner date for which we left the office early at 8:00 pm. I had bought a car now, but she always forced me to go in her car. She had reserved a table in a romantic place. She ordered some Thai food and I ordered Gujarati food that I had not eaten in a long time.

"Papa is organizing a party next Monday."

"I know he had discussed with me the promotional party of his new FMCG company; he has been working on it for a long time."

"He is going to announce..." Her lips smiled and eyes gleamed. She was blushing.

"What?"

"It will be a surprise announcement!"

"Stop throwing riddles."

"I am not going to tell you."

"OK, don't tell me." I ignored her excitement.

"You are so rude!" She pulled my plate away. I did not react and took another plate; I was relishing her irritation. She pulled the other plate too and punched my chest.

"Let me eat; I have worked a lot and I am hungry now."

She put the plate back and emptied the food on my plate, "Here eat and we will talk after you finish it all."

She was getting really irritated and angry. I had to give in, "OK, what is the surprise for me in the party?"

"I am not going to say anything." Now she was really putting up a show and enjoying it too.

"Please, sweetheart, tell me the surprise; I am dying to hear it."

"No not good enough. You will have to do better to please me." I gently touched her chin, moved her to me, our eyes locked together.

"If you will not tell me, I will kiss the owner of these beautiful eyes, whose lips are like rose petals and face is gleaming like the full moon." I went closer and closer to her with each word; when I was just few inches away from her lips, she brought her hand chirpily between us, "You are too much. This is a public place and people are watching us. He is going to announce our engagement that day. We are to exchange rings in the party."

I tried my best to look happy but a hesitation flickered in my eyes.

"You are not happy with the news?"

"I am happy; I was just wondering how swiftly things are moving."

"Yes, he has taken a big decision without your consent. He should have asked you."

"But you are a big mouthed girl" I grinned and taunted her which lightened up the environment.

We enjoyed the dinner but when I reached home, I sensed I was not as happy as I should be.

****

Section 3

Ponytail: The Love for Revenge

After all this was all that I wanted after working obsessively for the past few decades. Now my plan was bearing fruit-the plan to own his daughter and then own his company; to bring him on the road and to make him beg for the life of his family.

Chapter 38

Few Years Ago...

I came back home happy and excited after appearing for my last junior level board. I found my home locked. My neighbour informed me that mother had an accident and father had gone to the hospital.

Mr. Mehta and Mr. Ramakrishna owned nefarious businesses in the city. They were involved in all types of crimes including smuggling, murder, fraud, rape and kidnapping. Their automobile business was the front to carry out these illegal activities. They had managed strong support by paying off few greedy politicians and some high ranked police officers. Papa had collected enough strong evidence against them.

They first tried to bribe papa but he refused, then they resorted to making threatening calls but still papa did not back off. He successfully got warrants against them. The two devils did the unthinkable-they now have tried to kill my mother. She was fighting for her life in the hospital.

I was waiting at the neighbour's house when the police van came. Crime Branch officers in civil dress had raided our home. They broke open the door and started search operations. Papa was informed about the raid; he had to rush home when his presence was needed in the hospital.

Mr. Mehta and Mr. Ramakrishna had planted cocaine in our home, and as a result my father was suspended. His bank accounts, cash, savings and house were seized; we were on the road within a day.

Doctors asked for one lakh rupees for an emergency operation to save mummy but father's savings and bank accounts were frozen. He had to sell our furniture and grandmother's paintings. By the time money was arranged, mummy had left the world. He could not bear the loss and died of severe heart attack instantly.

After few months, Papa was proved innocent and our home was handed over to me. Papa had few honest friends in police department who helped to prove his innocence. They supported me in my studies and took care of my requirements. Papa had enough savings that supported me financially.

When I lit my parents' pyres, the fire of revenge ignited in my head. As a ritual I had to get my head shaved. I recalled Chanakya, who had taken the oath not to tie his 'Shikha' until the time he had exacted his revenge. Like Chanakya, I too was thirsting for revenge. I decided to become the richest and the most powerful man and then to destroy these two men. To keep the fire of revenge burning I took the oath not to cut my hair short. My long hair might have meant different things to people but to me they meant revenge for my parents' death.

I worked hard to grow my business-money and

power was everything to me. Girls could not distract me from my goal. I had good contacts with politicians and police officers. I built good public reputation and was one of the promising businessmen in the country.

The bird flew into the trap itself. Tapasya was the daughter of Mr. Ramakrishna. I hired her and trapped her in my love. In the drama of love, I started liking her but I never forgot the revenge. I proposed marriage to her which she accepted. Everything was working according to the plan. Partnership with Kaumudi was also part of my plan to take revenge. I knew Tapasya's possessiveness for me and accordingly worked out a plan. I arranged for her to receive photos of me with Mahek. She reacted expectedly and left home in anger. I had hired few thugs to kill her. The killing was made to look like suicide. I was called by the police to identify the body. I identified the body based on the outfit she was wearing. The body was handed over to her father, Mr. Ramakrishna. As planned I did not want to meet him that time.

Although I was happy with my revenge but it made me sad too. Tapasya was a good human and she loved me. But the fire of revenge had turned into an inferno. I had decided to take away everything dear to Mehta and Ramakrishna.

Everything was meticulously planned that nobody suspected me-not even Ahmad. Mr.

Ramakrishna might have suspected me but the one-year withdrawal from the world was enough for him to remove any suspicion of my involvement.

I withdrew myself from business, because I was hurt by myself and also I wanted to think through to the second stage of my revenge. I did detailed background check of Mr. Mehta's business. After establishing his business with the illegal money, he was now doing legitimate business ever since he broke up with Mr. Ramakrishna. Both of them had left the world of crime and were leading straight lives.

The fire of revenge inside me kept raging. My blood bubbled every time I heard their names. These two had blood on their hands and my revenge was still incomplete.

****

Chapter 39

"May we come in, Mr. Prabuddh?" Mahavirji knocked on the door. I was checking mails in my drawing room. I had hung out with Mahavirji's group several times in the society garden after our first meeting. This was the first time they had come to my home. I wondered why.

"Welcome Mahavirji and Rajendraji, please come in." I put the laptop aside and greeted them.

"We did not see you last week so we thought we will catch you at home." As usual Mahavirji was the spokesperson.

"I was busy with work. Can I get you something-tea or coffee? You are visiting my home for the first time."

"No thanks, we just had tea. We are here to invite you." Mahavirji paused and looked at Rajendra.

"Every year we plan a culture week in our society when various activities like sports, dances, quizzes, antakshari take place. This year the culture week is planned starting from Sunday. Please keep yourself free this Sunday as you are the chief guest at the opening ceremony."

"Oh thanks a lot. I am honoured! Of course I will love to attend. Just a minute please." I was not sure if they were soliciting donations. I knew such events required financial support.

"Mahavirji, I would like to contribute some money. Please let me know how much do you need." I was ready with pen and cheque book.

"Prabuddh, you sensed our need without us telling you. The society committee's budget for the event is short of seventy-five thousand rupees.

"I think one and half lakh will be better. Please arrange something for the children if possible." I wrote the cheque in the name of society committee and handed it over to Mahavirji.

****

Chapter 40

"What are you going to wear in the opening ceremony tomorrow?" Amita asked me on Saturday evening as I wolfed down a Mexican dish she had recently learned and prepared.

"I have not decided."

"I and Patanjali are going to wear sarees."

"Nice, you will make people go crazy." I was trying to chew something hard.

"You should try some ethnic wear too. You will look great in it."

"What is this? It tastes different." I was still trying to figure out what I was chewing.

"Don't change the topic. And what will you do with your hair?"

"You are boring me."

"You should try different hairstyle like bun or French braid."

"Amita, I am not in the mood to discuss these things. I don't even know if I am attending the function or not."

"Why-what happened?"

"Mr. Mehta is going to announce our engagement. I and Kaumudi are going to be engaged

149

on Monday."

Her eyes could not hide her sadness. "I forgot to serve your favourite *shrikhand*." She rose and went to the kitchen. I knew she went to the kitchen not only to bring *shrikhand* but also to wipe her tears. She had started to love me but I could not decide whether I loved Amita or not.

Everything was complicated for me; first Tapasya to whom I proposed marriage and now I was going to be engaged to Kaumudi. It was all for revenge only. I was in love with Tapasya but she was not in the world anymore.

But Amita was more than a friend. I felt comfortable in her presence. Perhaps I loved her. Starting with affection, she had made her own space in my heart.

She returned with my favorite *'Kesar Shrikhand'*. She knew everything about me-my tastes, my likes, dislikes, my moods and changes in moods. She knew all my secrets.

I was enjoying the shrikhand. Amita looked disturbed.

"Amita, I am sorry but..."

"Sorry for what?"

"I should have told you this before."

"You should not be sorry. I knew about your relationship with Kaumudi. I was a fool who was thinking…" Her throat choked up.

"Amita, I don't know for sure but I have feelings for you too."

"And where is my number in that long line Mr. Prabuddh? Stop playing this game with me." She was annoyed.

"I really mean; perhaps I …"

"Stop! I know you use that line with every girl you meet. How many girls have heard this line before?" She chided me. I went quiet. She continued to speak. "You have used girls for your selfish motives only. My mother had told me that your father had great respect for women; but you are quite different. You have always played with feelings of girls and for what? For bloody business and money only. First you played with Tapasya, then Kaumudi and now me. You should be ashamed of yourself." The situation had gone out of my hands. I could not stay any longer. She realized what she had done-she had expressed her insecurity.

She was about to burst into tears when I kissed her lips. She trembled with anger. "Amita I am not going to get engaged with Kaumudi. And yes that is right; I loved Tapasya, I loved Kaumudi and I love you too. And my love is true for all; the only thing I cannot decide is who I should marry. I don't want to do injustice to anyone. It is also true that Tapasya is my first love and nobody will be able to take her place."

She was shivering and confused. Then I rose to leave. "Tomorrow you will see the real me. I will meet you in the morning. Please be ready wearing your best saree." She smiled finally.

****

Chapter 41

Ahmad was calling me on my cell phone. We had planned an important discussion on Prajwalit Ltd. I disconnected his call and texted him that I will call him tomorrow.

Something was distracting me. I was having trouble focusing on my work and on my goal.

I had been lying on the bed for an hour but could not sleep. My mind was a whirlpool of thoughts. I looked at the time. It was midnight. I went to the main hall and switched on the television. My mind did not go silent even after surfing the channels for half an hour.

An idea flashed in my mind. I sat in the 'Padmasan' position before the wall, on which the Painting 'City Boy in the Forest' was hanging. Amita had gifted me my grandmother's painting. I closed my eyes and started to breath slowly. I was practicing meditation for the first time at night to calm down my mind and stop these thoughts so that I could sleep soundly. Gradually I concentrated on my breathing. The breathing was rhythmic, deep and slow. I could feel the air moving in me; passing through each and every cell of my body. I could feel the air flowing out of my nose and ejecting all negative thoughts out of my body. With every breath my mind was becoming relaxed and calm.

I was lost in the space; the space that was

surrounded by snowy mountains. I could see a light at the top of the mountain. I went near it. The light was from a man I knew very well; he was my papa. His peaceful face had an eternal smile. My mind turned peaceful.

"Prabuddh, love makes the world not revenge. Revenge only destroys the world and spreads negativity in the world. Whatever happened to us was the decision of God, and we do not have any right to punish the humans behind that. We should never forsake humanity and goodness. Engulfed in the fire of revenge you have lost so much; your desire to seek revenge hurts me. If you really want to see me happy, forget revenge and accept the love."

The light disappeared; I could feel warmth on my eyelids. The sun had started to rise. A new Sunday morning dawned with infinite peace. The soft golden light of the sun was coming through the window and falling on my eyes.

After a long time, I had a marathon morning meditation. In the session, I interacted with my papa who showed me the path; the path of truth, love and happiness. He urged me to give up the feelings of revenge and to embrace the love present in the world-love spreads peace in the world while revenge begets hatred.

****

Chapter 42

"Cut them short, very short." I was seated in the chair of the Hairline Salon at 8:00 am Sunday morning. The hairdresser girl was standing behind me amazed and smiling.

"Are you sure? It must have taken lots of effort to grow this long and beautiful hair."

"I am sure; please cut them short."

"I can give you other hairstyles that will look much better on you, and you will not have to cut them this short."

"I don't have much time; please do as I tell you."

"OK Sir! Your choice."

The sound of scissors and comb sounded like music to me. The hairdresser's hands were moving efficiently over my head; trimmers, scissors and comb-I had short hair in fifteen minutes.

I looked in the mirror; the short hair made my face look different. It has been about more than ten years since I last saw myself with such short hair. It seemed I was relieved of a burden that I had been carrying for years.

After returning to home from salon, I did my daily rituals and took bath.

In no time, I was ready in my Indian dress of kurta and pajama. I dressed like my Papa who wore similar attire when he attended social functions. The opening ceremony of the annual function of the society was scheduled for 9:00 am.

I knocked at Amita's door.

"Come in, Prabuddh!" She shouted. The girls were standing in the hall fussing with their sarees and getting their looks right. None of them looked at me. "We are ready, just a minute." Finally Amita saw me. She froze in shock, her mouth fell down and her eyes bulged out. Patanjali gave the same reaction. Then they both burst into laughter. I stood there embarrassed.

"That's enough, let us go; we are getting late."

"We don't believe our eyes! You have cut your hair. Someone must have told you to do so; must be your girlfriend." Patanjali chuckled.

I looked at Amita and she turned red hearing the word 'girlfriend'. Patanjali did not fail to catch the reaction in our eyes.

"Amita is that girlfriend you? Oh my God!" Patanjali wondered.

"None of your business; we are getting late, let us go." Amita ended the discussion and hurried to the door.

Amita must be having butterflies in her stomach. But the reason for me cutting my hair was altogether different. I had decided to start with a clean slate and disclose all truth.

After having lunch at the ceremony, all members dispersed to meet again in the evening for the Antakshari competition.

"Amita, I want to tell you something." I

approached her when she was alone in the passage on the way to her apartment.

"Yes, Prabuddh!" Her eyes could not hide her inner happiness.

"Not here, you need to come with me."

"Right now?"

"Yes, it is really important."

"Ok, will you let me change?"

"I don't think you need to."

"Sometimes you really act weird. Nobody can understand you." I was in cheerful mood and did not mind what she was saying. Although I was stressed somewhat with the situation I would have to face after few minutes.

I had planned to disclose everything. I did not know what the reactions would be. I had prepared myself for the worst case scenario-even being handed over to the police and tried for murder. I was expecting forgiveness from Kaumudi for reasons I did not know. I felt Amita should also hear the truth, so I had asked her to come with me. We both sat in my car and before I could crank the engine, I got a call from a local landline number.

****

Chapter 43

Few hours back ....

In the morning, I had called Mr. Ramakrishna, Kaumudi and Mr. Mehta. I had asked them all to assemble at Mr. Ramakrishna's house in the afternoon as I had to disclose some important information about Tapasya's death. Mr. Ramakrishna had confirmed few minutes ago that he had gone personally to pick up both Mr. Mehta and Kaumudi. Now they were all on their way to Mr. Ramakrishna's house.

Ramakrishna was driving the car as various thoughts overwhelmed his mind. Mr. Mehta was seated beside him and Kaumudi sat on the rear seat.

"Why has Prabuddh called us together? What does he want to tell us about Tapasya?" Mr. Mehta broke the heavy silence.

"Even I don't know; he just told me that he wanted to disclose something about Tapasya." Ramakrishna was just as unaware of the reason like the others.

"Kaumudi did he tell you anything?" Mr. Mehta asked.

"No, he did not tell me anything. I called him again but he asked me to wait until afternoon."

The confusion and tension was increasing in the car. Mr. Ramakrishna stepped on the pedal as the traffic was quite low on the roads of Delhi.

The speedometer hit the ninety mark.

"Rama calm down and slow down the car, we have enough time to get there. This could be dangerous." Mr. Mehta warned his friend.

"It is OK, Mehta. There is nobody on the roads and I drive safe." Mr. Ramakrishna justified his speed. "Let's listen to some music." Ramakrishna was distracted while turning on the radio. A cyclist appeared from nowhere trying to cross the road.

"Uncle look out!" Kaumudi screamed. Ramakrishna reflexively pulled at the steering and with brakes screeching saved the cyclist but the speeding car jumped the divider unto incoming traffic.

Death in the form of a heavy truck struck the wayward car head-on. The momentum of the truck threw the car into the air pulverizing it. The air was filled with screams and there was blood everywhere. The truck sped off the site of accident. All three occupants of the car had severe head injuries. Someone called the PCR van.

****

Chapter 44

"Hello!"

"Am I speaking to Mr. Prabuddh?"

"Yes you are."

"Mr. Prabuddh, I am calling from the city hospital. We have a patient named Miss Kaumudi along with two others. We have managed to find your number from their phones. They have been involved in an accident and are in serious condition. You need to come to the city hospital right away

"I am coming." I went numb. I could not believe what I had just heard. Amita asked me about the call. I was lost and my mind went blank.

After a minute I got hold of myself. I told her about the tragic news and we drove to the hospital. Mr. Ramakrishna and Mr. Mehta had already left the world when we reached there. Kaumudi was in the operation theatre.

The operation went on for a long time.

"Sorry Mr. Prabuddh, we could not save the two men. The lady has brain hemorrhage. Although we have operated on her but her condition is still critical." The doctor informed me regretfully. Mrs. Mehta and ex-wife of Mr. Ramakrishna had arrived hearing the news.

Mrs. Mehta could not bear the news of the death

of her husband. She suffered a heart attack. The doctors tried to revive her but she died.

Kaumudi's operation was successful and she regained her consciousness after coming out of the effects of anesthesia. I rushed to Kaumudi.

She smiled when she saw me and tried to get up even in her critical condition. She did not know about the sad demise of her parents. The doctor had told us to keep the news to ourselves until she was completely out of danger.

"Please don't get up Kaumudi. Doctor has told me that you will be all right in a few days. You are out of danger." My eyes had moistened.

"Where are Daddy and Uncle? How are they?" She was breathless while speaking.

"Don't speak; the doctor has asked you to rest." Amita approached her bed. Kaumudi smiled when she saw Amita. She read our faces. "They have left the world-right?"

Our silence gave away the sad news. She could not cry loudly but her eyes welled up. I took her hand and reassured her, "Kaumudi, be brave. They have lived good lives and enjoyed their time here. They have left the world happy."

She was staring at me. After a pause she asked me to come near her and whispered in my ears, "Why did you cut your hair?"

"It is a long story; I will tell you but first you need to recover."

"Where is Mom?" I went quiet. She could not bear my silence. Her eyes implored me to tell her.

"She has gone with your papa." I could not keep the news secret anymore. She closed her eyes as tears streamed over her cheeks wetting her pillow. I caressed her hair moving my hand over her head.

She opened her eyes and burst into tears and cried loudly. I took her in my arms and tried to console her. Amita also tried her best to comfort her.

Kaumudi controlled herself and looked at Amita. "Amita, will you do me a favor?"

Amita nodded.

"Prabuddh loves me and he loved Tapasya too; but I know he loves you the most."

"Kaumudi please stop and take some rest." Amita tried to stop Kaumudi.

"He is a very good man. He disclosed everything to me today early morning-about his parents, my father, uncle and Tapasya and also his motive behind his love for me and Tapasya." She paused.

"Now I am leaving this world. You have to take care of him." Amita's eyes were also full of tears.

Amita nodded, "Kaumudi, Prabuddh is yours and will always remain yours."

Kaumudi smiled and put my hand into Amita's hand and closed her eyes. She stopped breathing and became motionless. Doctors on call rushed in.

Everything turned into a blur. The world went quiet for me. I could not speak or hear anything. All I could see was Kaumudi who was not responding to resuscitation. The monitor line went straight. The doctor came to me, put his hands on my shoulder and told me something. I could not hear what he said. I went to her and tried to wake her up. I kissed her and shook her.

I promised to spend my entire time with her but she did not respond.

I realized she had left me alone. I was alone in this world. I cursed God for snatching everyone I loved- my parents, Tapasya and now Kaumudi.

****

Five years later...

"Amita, how much time will you take? We are getting late for the award function." I was to be recognized with the 'Businessman of the Year' award that evening and Amita was taking time to get ready in our new villa on the outskirts of Delhi.

Chapter 45

In those five years…

Mr. Mehta and Mr. Ramakrishna had willed their property to me; I developed a trust from the money headed by Amita; for welfare of children. The trust was for financial and educational help of any children all over the India. 89 high class orphanages and 55 world class schools were built from the fund for favor of orphan children.

Prajwalit Ltd. Was chaired by Ahmad and Dr. Arpan was successful to run his own pharmaceutical company.

I was still hard worker and good businessman and spent sufficient time with my family. Amita gifted me two little angels the very next year I married her; Amita suggested we name them Tapasya and Kaumudi. At last my life was peaceful; I was successful businessman, husband and a good father.

And that evening was to be awarded as 'Businessman of the year'. Amita adored her beauty with pink saree and classic make up. In no time, we were on the way to the awardee function; populated by industrialists, politicians, media and other eminent personalities.

My two little angels accompanying were sleepy after dinner; so Amita left the function with two girls in my car. I had to meet other delegated for business purpose so I continued in the function. I denied her proposal to send car back after reaching home.

At 12 of night I was waving hands for the cab on wide black roads of Delhi; to my luck a cab stopped near me. I jumped in the cab as the driver agreed to drop me my home. Melodious songs from his radio were only disturbance in the heavy deep silence.

The cab was flowing on the road smoothly and a consistent speed; absence of traffic at the time amazed me and the driver also at the time. I had never seen Delhi sleeping in such a peace before; I knew the city always crowded, fast and running.

Cab was suddenly stopped without any visible reason. The frightened driver glanced back from the rear mirror and then jumped out of the cab; he was confused looking here and there. After a minute, he returned to cab.

"Nothing Sirji, I had to break to save lady standing ahead of the car; but in a moment, there was none."

"Such illusions are common in mid-night; you may have confused flash of street light with human shadow."

It was not illusion only; she was Tapasya. She was with me when the shocked driver was searching her outside the car. The memory of her, and her soul always with me since my marriage. I was shocked also when I had seen her soul first time in my marriage. She was sitting with Amita and participating each ritual of marriage; I ignored it considering illusion of my tired brain. But it was not so, my marriage was also with her in the manner and after that she was always with me; without speaking a single word.

Amita took me to psychiatrist when I had told her about Spirit of Tapasya first time; and I never took medicine prescribed by the doctor. I felt useless to talk about her after that.

Tapasya would appear from anywhere staring me whenever she wanted; in business gatherings, during lunch, cinema hall, also in my bed room. She always slept in between me and Amita. I had taken her presence granted; she was harmless. Sometimes her presence gave me the support especially in business meeting. She never spoke a single word; just kept staring me. I would just close my eyes when I could not bear her quizzing gaze. She had been always in my memory and I could never decide whether it was illusion or reality.

"Congratulations Prabuddh" she spoke first time long after five years.

She came near to me and kissed me, my short hairs grew longer and turned into ponytail; when she was kissing me. Her hands were surfing my hairs. I merged in her kiss with closed eyes.

"Let's go for long walk; it is time to reach our destiny, Prabuddh!" I could not resist anything she said; even I did not remember when I was out of the cab.

I did not care the cab driver frightened and shivering outside the car; the police van coming to the cab. I just glanced back to the police officers inspecting my dead body. I clenched her hand tightly; hugged her and walked with her light hearted and smiling.

****

Only love is Eternal

Follow the author

twitter.com/@prajjawalit2015

Email him: ontheearthbyprajjawalit@gmail.com

Facebook: https://www.facebook.com/pradipchauhan

To get published contact us on
contact@hrcpublisher.com

Hrcpublisher.in

Other titles from the pen of Author

Love stories

On the earth: In light of the sun